The Vampire Hunter's Academy

Book I

The Darkness

In memory of the first and only author

Whose writing will live forever in my heart...

Whose characters not only took my breath away...

Whose storylines encouraged me to put pen to paper

And...

Whose message which was written and hidden in plain sight

Has been received

You encouraged your readers to stay in the Light

I now bathe in it...

R.I.P. Leslie Esdale Banks

The opportunity to meet you never arrived

But somehow, you knew me....

-Delizhia D. Jenkins

Books by Delizhia D. Jenkins

Nubia Rising: The Awakening

Love at Last

Blind Salvation (The Dark Royals Series)

Viper

Sin: Daughter of the Grim Reaper

In the Light of Darkness: The Grey Chronicles of Dawn

Coming Soon

Viper Returns

Sin: Daughter of the Grim Reaper Book 2

Into the Shadows

Escape

The Family Curse

Prologue

Sixteen years ago...

The convening of dark forces could be felt throughout the halls of the most powerful and influential church in the world-the Vatican. Hidden in secrecy in a secured room, the Pope himself possessed no knowledge of the Guardian sect that protected the human race from the complete and total darkness. Only twelve of them were able to make the trek from whatever part of the globe they originated from for this precise moment. For centuries, members of this secret order watched and waited for the birth of the prophesized Akhkharu Alal: huntress, slayer, destroyer of demons; and for centuries they prepared. Many slayers had come and gone since the birth of man, when evil first made its presence known on the earth realm. But this particular slayer would be the first of her kind born in over two thousand years...and this slayer would be sent to tip the balance of scales in favor of the Light. She would be the strongest ever born and it was foretold that she would lead the thousands of guardians in a final battle between the Light and the Dark. The stars never lied and it was on this night on September 3rd, that her presence had been announced in the sky, written in a starry language that only a highly trained astrologer could read. As all twelve guardians, ranging in age from 19-86, male and female sat around the marble table in front of a large book made of its original papyrus leaves and etched with writing varying from Akkadian, Kemetian, Egyptian, Chinese, and all of the other languages of old, each one of them held a look of concern in his or her eyes...The location of this Slayer had not been revealed, perhaps even the Light did not trust even the guardians who swore the sacred oath to protect her at any and every cost. Time was of serious essence. There was only a window of 21 years before the Darkness would come for her; and in 21 years she would need to be taught everything she would need to know to not only protect herself, but to protect mankind from the forces of evil.

A single thought was shared among the brethren: they would scatter the globe in search of the huntress and in the meantime, they would continue to scout and train potential guardians at the top secret yet highly selective academy. In 21 years, not only will she begin her mission, but she must choose seven of the finest and most trust worthy warriors to protect and aid her in her quest against the ultimate darkness. The Guardians reviewed the pages of the book one last time before it was returned to its mysterious location. The etched symbols blazed a white hot silver glow, providing only one clue to who the new huntress happened to be in a single name: Sanaya.

. . . .

October 2015…

Sanaya Scott watched her mother sit by the window sill, Jack Daniel's in one hand and a cigarette in another. Her father had yet to come home, and whenever her mother had a bottle of liquor in hand, she knew things weren't good. Patrice hadn't said a word since she'd come home from a long day at the post office, and Sanaya knew something wasn't right. As a matter of fact, she'd been walking on eggshells around her mother all week since her father, Roland, went away to the store and never came back. Patrice had yet to file a missing person's report, being that this would not be the first time Roland disappeared without a trace. Sanaya sighed, secretly wishing some self-esteem was at the bottom of the liquor bottle so that her mother would just divorce him and move on. The man was a cheater and showed no signs of changing any time soon. Sanaya assumed that he had always been that way, but could not figure out for the life of her why her mother would put up with it. The last time he disappeared, he ran off with one of Patrice's ex-friends for two years before coming home with his tail between his legs. For the first six months after his departure, she had to live with her Aunt Shawna while her mother struggled through a serious bout of depression and drinking. After she almost drank herself to the point of a coma, she finally began to clean herself up, found a new job at the post office as a clerk, and things began to look up for

Sanaya and Patrice. Until her dad came home, and well…things went downhill from there. And now, they were back in the shit hole.

Sanaya crept into the kitchen, trying to block out her mother's thoughts, which was another thing: she could actually hear what people were thinking as they were thinking, something that at one point, freaked her out. She smoothed the fine hairs that framed her face back into the freshly flat ironed ponytail she could feel bouncing against the back of her neck as she stealthily opened the fridge.

This son of a bitch got me all the way fucked up, her mother seethed mentally, still staring out of the window. *As soon as he comes back, I'm leaving his ass and he can see for himself what it's like to raise a child alone…*

Sanaya quickly grabbed her left over foot long sandwich from Subway her mother picked up for her after school, and headed back to her room while she could. If Patrice caught wind of her moving about the house in the state that she was in, Sanaya would have to bear the verbal brunt of her mother's tirade until it was time for her to get to school.

Fuck him!

Sanaya gently eased the door to her room shut and cut the volume down just low enough not to disturb her mother… As of late, her hearing had become much more sensitive and acute that even at the television's lowest volume, it still sounded like her ear drums were going to explode. As a matter of fact, since she was twelve her senses had heightened to the realms of abnormal. She could see things at least a mile away with total clarity, all the way down to the most minute detail. She could smell with equal acuity, having spent many a day in the nurse's office for extreme nausea and vomiting from the nasal sensitivity. One time after being picked up from school for vomiting, her mother asked her if she was pregnant, and drove her to a local free clinic where she was forced to take a pregnancy test despite her still being a virgin.

She hid most of the changes that took place within her body other than the typical issues that all females went through as they transitioned into young adulthood; but everything else such as the heightened sensitivity to her environment, and the awareness of the ever present feeling of something darker, and stronger than herself, she kept locked away. Besides, her mother had other issues to worry about besides the fact that her daughter's developing "gifts" should have by rights placed her in the nut house. She learned a long time ago that there just wasn't room for special people like her,and whatever these gifts are…well, there is no such thing as super heroes. Those characters only existed in the pages of a Marvel comic books.

Sanaya tightened the strings of her berry pink pajama bottoms and plopped on her twin sized bed, decorated with a purple comforter set, and covered with stuffed animals she collected since she was old enough to walk. Yeah, it was childish but how else would she sleep at night when she always felt like someone was watching her?

Taking a bite of the leftover Philly cheese steak sub, she listened for her mother, happy to have distanced herself from her mother's toxic thoughts, but dreading what the night may bring from Patrice's drunken stupor. Sanaya finished her sandwich and tossed the wrapping into her purple waste bin by the door before crawling into bed. Patrice would more than likely sit by the window all night if left undistracted from her thoughts, which Sanaya intended to do. Sanaya wrestled underneath the welcoming comfort of her covers, and allows her thoughts to drift to the sound of MTV's Cribs, and the hauntingly eerie silence which begun to blanket her street. She shrugged off the horrifying sensation as paranoia, and cursing herself for never being able to relax.

She grabbed the remote and cut the television off and just listened. She heard the sound of her father's 2002 Honda Civic pull up into the driveway of their two storied duplex. The hum of the engine came to a stop as he stepped out onto the pavement, his heavy footsteps tapping against the pavement. Her whole body tensed as she listened to the jingle of his keys clink against the metal door. Something wasn't right…she did not know how she knew, but something deep inside of her told her something about her father's return just wasn't right. She detected the presence of someone else just outside of her home's iron gate, and she sat up quickly; her eyes adjusting to the dark as if it were day. She listened intently, tuning more into what may have been going on outside than in.

The presence moved through the shadows with the stealth and agility of a trained assassin before coming to a stop just underneath her bedroom window. She got up to take a peek when she could hear her mother's drunken outburst slam into her cranium.

"So which bitch was it this time, Roland?" she demanded.

Sanaya could see it in her mind's eye: her mother leaning against the wooden dining room table with a multicolored scarf on her head full of tightly coiled locks she kept hidden under various wigs; her large brown eyes tinged with red from hours of crying and drinking; her once beautifully smooth brown skin marred with worry lines and few wrinkles here and there; her 5'9" frame draped in an old tattered red robe, and all signs of hope and happiness completely drained from her pores. Standing before her father was a shell of a woman who lacked the one thing she wanted most in the world: the love of her husband.

Sanaya listened for her father's reply, which came out in a melodic echo that caused her skin to prickle.

"You've been drinking," was all he said.

Hearing her father's voice made something within her snap, and she mentally shot her mother a message: *Run mama!*

However, the message fell on deaf ears because her mother instantly began her verbal tirade, belting out curses, threats and everything else she could think of. Sanaya quietly eased the door open and slid out, and crept down the hall, cautious to remain hidden in the shadows, careful not to be seen by the version of the man she knew as her father. All of her instincts began to fire off the instant she laid eyes on her father. He looked like Roland, sounded like Roland, and said things that Roland would say, but Sanaya shuddered… Roland wasn't Roland.

She peered out just in time to witness her mother slap her father with a force that should have knocked the wind out of him, but he never staggered. He never flinched. He just glared at her with such intensity, that even in her drunken and enraged state, Patrice took a step back. That is when Sanaya noticed the difference. Roland's mouth crested with two pointed teeth that were as thick as switch blades and equally as sharp, which extended to near the end of his jawline. His normally hazel brown eyes flickered with a deep crimson, and his honey brown skin appeared more ashen and dull.

Patrice took another step back, unsure of which direction to go, and Roland continued to stalk after her.

"Get the hell away from me Roland," Patrice warned. "I mean it."

"Or else what?" Roland asked coolly.

No longer able to sit back and wait for her father to seal her mother's fate, Sanaya sprang to her feet, armed only with her bravery and fear for her mother's life, she charged at her father, only for him to knock her into the wall with the sweep of his hand. Her head connected with the 8 x 12 mirror her mother insisted on purchasing from Ross a year ago, before she collapsed to the ground.

"Sanaya!" Patrice called out, her back now pinned against the cupboard and her husband's face just inches away from hers.

"I am terribly glad to be rid of you, you miserable…useless…bitch," Roland articulated slowly. "I long ago grew tired of your endless ramblings…" He leaned in closer. "And to answer the question you begged of me long ago, yes, your sister is better."

Patrice's gasp was followed by her scream as Roland slammed her into the cupboard and sank his teeth into her throat. Sanaya, dazed and bloodied, struggled to get to her feet, when the window from which her mother gazed out into the night shattered, and the watchful presence emerged, dressed in all black and armed with a long sword and a mission, burst through the shattered window. With the speed and agility of a panther, the hooded assassin's sword sliced through the air with a chime, taking Roland's head clean off of his shoulders. Patrice's body slumped to the floor, her hands clutching her throat.

Sanaya managed to get on her feet, forcing herself to stumble to her mother's aid. Slightly dazed, she inched closer drawing in deep breaths as she watched her mother spew up her own blood. Kneeling beside her, she brought her mother's head to her chest, unsure of what to do or who to turn to. The hooded assassin, still clutching the sword approached them, pulling out a small vial of clear liquid and removing the spongy cap. Before Sanaya could respond, the assassin sprinkled a few drops of the mystery fluid onto her mother and the instant the drop made contact, her mother began to incinerate.

"What the fuck did you do to her?" Sanaya sobbed jumping back, as her mother screamed and thrashed about as her body became consumed with flames.

The hooded assassin regarded her with a disinterested stare before returning to Patrice's body, as it slowly turned to a pile of ash. Patrice's screams abated, her arms no longer thrashing about as the flames continued to consume her. Sanaya's sobs became louder as she fell to her knees once more. Whatever her father had done, he'd brought it home to her mother. and nowboth of her parents were gone. Overwrought with grief, she buried her face in her hands, not expecting the sudden strike of a small dart to the base of her neck. She flinched, and scrambled to her feet to address the sudden threat. However, the specially calibrated toxin sent a shock to her nervous system and the last thing she remembered was the heavy hand of the hooded assassin catching her by the waist before her face hit the floor.

CHAPTER 1

One year later...

Sanaya moved like poetry in motion as she gracefully bent her knees, folding her upper torso just inches above the ground just as the actors did in the movie, The Matrix, dodging the round of bullets flying in her direction. She back flipped quickly out of range from an arrow with her name on it. Her trainers showed no mercy, and neither would the creatures she was destined to hunt upon graduating from the academy. Without turning around, she nailed her opponent in the nose with an elbow. Sensing the moment he went down, she spun on her heels to go in for the kill. Consumed with bloodlust and rage, she reached for the six inch dagger she kept at her waist when Archer rung the bells, an indicator for her to stop. But she would not stop. Never again would she fall victim to...

"Sanaya!" Archer yelled. He was on his feet in a flash and just in time to grab Sanaya's wrist, forcing her to drop the blade. "What are you doing? He's done! Didn't you hear the bells?"

Sanaya snatched her wrist away from him and stepped back. Her opponent, Ryder, a senior student, was curled in a fetal position on the floor, his face in his palms and blood everywhere. She inhaled deeply in an attempt to normalize her senses. She had no idea what happened. Ryder had done absolutely nothing to provoke her like the other students did her first week. But something else had come over her. Had Archer not stepped in when he did...

"I-I-I don't know what happened..." She stammered. Realizing what she had almost done, Sanaya mentally began to freak out.

"Take a walk. Your powers are developing faster than what we expected. Ryder will be taken to the medical unit, but he should be fine."

Sanaya stomped off, shoving the heavy double doors open of the gym, headed for the grassy area of the courtyard. She could feel the eyes of her peers on her back, but no one dared to mutter a word. Archer, of course, would find her. However, her best friend would be unavailable for a venting session for the next few hours. Of course, this little incident would isolate her even more from the rest of the student body. Thankfully the courtyard was empty. All of the hundred or so students or "Guardians in Training," were in one of the various classes required to be recognized as a hunter. Sanaya, on the other hand, was here at the academy for an entirely different purpose. According to Archer, and the entire Catholic Church, she is what the ancient Babylonians described as the *Akhkharu Alal: Akhkharu* meaning *vampire* and *Alal* meaning *Destroyer*. There were many more like her that had come and gone. However, she is the most recent and theorized to be the strongest of vampire hunters ever born. What made matters worse, is that her parents never knew what she was. As a matter of fact, her mother never knew about her abilities because Sanaya had made it a point to hide them well,and now, here at the academy, she would be under heavy guard until it was time for her to hunt. Here, she would learn everything a vampire huntress is supposed to know about vampires, demons, werewolves and other supernatural entities that the Darkness sent to terrorize the human populations. Here, her skills and abilities would be developed and tested beyond her limits. Here, she would fit in with other teens and young adults possessing abilities that labeled them as "freaks" in the human world, and here, when the time came, she would be allowed to personally select her team of guardians; specialized warriors destined to follow her lead as they eradicate the forces of darkness, who would go into the world with her as was required, protecting her as she would protect humanity... Being here at the Academy just made her feel more alone and isolated than ever.

She took a seat on the gigantic roots of the lone Willow tree she mentally claimed as hers. Under the cover of its branches, she found peace, could gather her thoughts, and remind herself that four years would come and go and she would be out of this place. Screw choosing her own team of Guardians. Half of them didn't like her anyways.

She stretched her long legs out onto the cool grass and rested her head against the trunk, and blew out a deep breath. It had been a year since her mother was killed by her father, who after going missing for a week, came home as a vampire, changing her fate forever. She closed her eyes and tried not to focus on that horrific night when she sensed the familiar presence of her guardian and personal trainer, Archer. She didn't need to say a word; she could just communicate with him telepathically. Besides, what could she say? She almost killed a classmate.

She met his hard brown eyed stare and sighed. *I don't know what came over me,* she shot to him telepathically.

He raised an eyebrow and tightened his lips. *I know… I think it's time you went hunting.*

Her eyes widened. *Seriously?*

Yep. You are too strong and pairing you with other classmates, despite their seniority, is too dangerous. These old heads who run the joint should know better, Archer shrugged. "Go clean yourself up. You have been excused from your classes for the rest of the day." He turned to leave but then stopped. "Oh, and your real training begins at midnight. Meet me here, and dress warm." Archer didn't bother to wait for her response as he departed back towards the gym. Sanaya watched his lean frame move with the confident strut of a peacock. Almost all of the teenaged girls had a crush on Archer; each of them daydreaming of the minute they would turn 18 and old enough to earn the affections of the Guardian, whose handsome face should have graced the covers of Calvin Klein and Givenchy ads.

Standing a little over 6'2" with an, and bronzed skin, Sanaya could see why he was the talk of the school. Unfortunately, Archer shared a link with her, as her primary guardian. Primary Guardians always shared a psychic link with the Slayers in their charge; it strengthened their bond. Archer could find Sanaya anywhere on the planet if he wanted to and vice versa. Therefore, the typical lustful teenaged thoughts about an older man was out of the question. Besides she had enough to concern herself with. She checked the time on her Walmart bought Timex watch: 1:32 p.m. Third period was just about over, and she knew the word would spread like wild fire about the incident with Ryder, which was all the more reason for her to beat feet to her room. She pulled out her Samsung Galaxy Note, courtesy of the Vatican (whom she was now officially under the care of,) sent a quick text to her best friend, Maya, before dusting off the bits of bark and leaves from her dark blue jeans, and used her ability to hyper speed her way to her room located on the far, western side of the campus, silently thanking the powers that be for her own private room. Some alone time would do her some justice right about now. Besides, she would be going on her first live hunt tonight, and she would need as much rest and mental clarity she could get.

CHAPTER TWO

Sanaya woke to the sound of hard knocking against her door. She groggily sat up, rubbed her eyes and pushed the comforter away from her body.

"Coming!" she shouted as she swung her feet over the edge of her twin bed and stumbled to the door.

"Sanaya! It is dinner time! Hurry up before they close the cafeteria!" Maya shouted behind the door.

Sanaya opened the door, but not in enough time before Maya pushed her way in almost knocking Sanaya off balance.

"I'm coming, damn Maya!" Sanaya grumbled as she went into her private bathroom and slipped on her jeans.

"Girl, I have been knocking for the last twenty minutes. Are you alright?" Maya plopped down on Sanaya's bed, tossing a thickly braided lock over her shoulder.

"Yeah, I'm good. Just tired..." Sanaya replied, slipping on a pair of her favorite black Nikes.

"I heard about what happened with Ryder..."

Sanaya groaned. "It was an accident."

"I know, and Ryder is ok. The medics fixed him up and he is as good as new. But they said your eyes changed. You had this crazy look like you were about to..."

"Bloodlust. That is what I felt, which is why Archer is taking me out hunting tonight."

Maya gasped. "For reals? Only senior students get to go out in the field-"

"Well, according to Archer it is too dangerous for even the most senior students to spar with me."

"Oh my gosh girl are you nervous?"

Sanaya slipped on a black hoodie and zipped it up before replying. "Scared shitless, but what else can I do?"

"Well, you are "The Chosen One'," Maya said making quotation signs with her hands.

Sanaya shrugged. "So? It doesn't mean I am not entitled to fear."

"Well, all I know is I better be the first one you select as a member of your guardian team when the time comes."

Sanaya smiled. "You know you got first dibs. Besides, you may be the only one I choose. You know most of these suckaz don't like me."

Maya sucked her teeth. "That's because they are jealous that you were born with the gifts and they weren't."

Sanaya wished it were that simple as she closed and locked the door to her room. However, she had already been inside the heads of some of the students who gave her the most grief, and the fact of the matter is, some of those so called future Guardians are just plain old evil on the inside. Some of them enjoyed making her life miserable because in some sick and twisted way, it made them feel better about their lots in life.

They walked quickly, Sanaya being careful to walk using a quickened human pace instead of hyper speed so that Maya could keep up. Maya was gifted like all of the students at the Academy. She was a strong clairvoyant born and raised in a voodoo brothel. Her mother was the high priestess, while her father had been some poor schmoe who was later sacrificed to one of the demon entities that the occult summoned to do their dirty work. Maya was supposed to replace her mother when the time came, however when she was nine Child Protective Services got involved and somehow her information was sent to the Vatican not long after she was safely removed from her mother's clutches and placed under the care and guidance of The Academy ever since. Sanaya was introduced to Maya during her second week of her stay with the Vatican. The two clicked and have been friends ever since.

The cafeteria closed at seven, and Sanaya checked her watch and discovered that they had about forty-five minutes to grab a plate and eat. They reached the hall ten minutes later, and Sanaya allowed Maya to stand in front of her to grab a plate to pick from the buffet styled dining room. All of the students were still seated, finishing up their typical teenaged dinner conversation with endless banter and laughter, filling the hall to maximum capacity with the noise level. She followed behind her friend, making sure to keep close and pretending to be occupied with the task at hand. Unfortunately, her attempt to remain inconspicuous failed, and it was not long before the awareness of her presence filled the room.

"Girl, all eyes are on you," Maya whispered, knowing Sanaya would hear her despite the noise.

"I know…but aren't they always?" Sanaya whispered back.

Maya spotted a vacant table nearest the exit and the two of them took a seat. Maya eyed Sanaya's scarce selections on her plate which included some watermelon, a couple of pieces of baked chicken breasts, a biscuit, and a blueberry muffin.

"Don't let these bitches get to you," Maya soothed, taking a bite of her pepperoni pizza.

Sanaya sighed. "I'm just tired of it, ya know? I didn't have to go through none of this at home…"

"I don't get what the big deal is anyway," Maya continued. "Plenty of kids got hurt during sparring. Ryder is not the first one or the last."

"I almost killed him Maya," Sanaya whispered looking down at her plate. "I had the knife in my hand, and had Archer not stopped me I would have killed him."

Maya didn't say anything more. The two of them shared a look, and Maya continued eating. Sanaya continued to telepathically survey the room, when she found herself and Maya's table surrounded by none other than Elizabeth Van Helsing and her crew of followers.

Sanaya didn't need to turn around to see who it was, and she remained facing Maya, purposely keeping her back to Elizabeth.

"Well look who decided to grace us with her presence," Elizabeth spat, narrowing her gaze on Maya. "You are fortunate you weren't kicked out and left to die on the street like the little street rat that you are for harming a student," she continued to taunt.

Maya's eyes met Sanaya's expressionless face. *Come on girl we can take her...I have been praying for a reason to knock this bitch out,* Maya mentally shot to her.

She won't fight me. She wants me to beat her up so I can get kicked out and she can go back to ruling the school. As much as I would love to beat her face in, my hands are tied.

Sanaya turned around to face Elizabeth, her eyes focused on the dark haired bully and alpha female of her group. "Don't you have something in a cauldron you should be brewing instead of attempting to bait me into something you couldn't handle?"

Elizabeth flinched as if she were ready to swing first, but one of her followers held her back. Sanaya didn't budge.

"Don't embarrass yourself Elizabeth. You and I both know you don't want none."

"Man, if you put hands on her its over for you, dog food," came the voice of Bradly, Elizabeth's so called boyfriend.

"Then tell your little bulldog to leave me the hell alone," Sanaya replied evenly.

"Bradly, get off of Elizabeth's nuts and grow your own," Maya retorted, rising from her seat, silently daring one of Elizabeth's flunkies to try something.

"I'm not scared of this little homeless cunt!" Elizabeth seethed, her midnight blue stare challenging Sanaya to react.

When Sanaya slowly rose from her seat, the entire room went quiet. Sanaya and Elizabeth stood eye to eye just inches away from each other. Feelings of repressed rage bubbled just beneath the surface of Sanaya's honey brown skin forcing something deep within Sanaya to snap. A calm, heavy hand landed on her shoulder snapping her out of the daze she was in, and she knew instinctively who the hand belonged to.

"What's going on ladies? Did someone lose a glass slipper?" Archer asked suspiciously, his hard gaze raking over Elizabeth and Sanaya, followed by Bradly, and the rest of the six teens who were led by the descendent of Van Helsing.

"Nothing is going on Archer," Sanaya said coolly. "Elizabeth and her pack of Dingoes were just leaving."

Elizabeth scowled and hesitated before throwing in the towel. She motioned for her crew to follow her, and they left the cafeteria without another word.

"The cafeteria is now closed!" Archer announced to the remaining students still sitting at the nearby tables. "The party is officially over! There is nothing new to see here and remember this is finals week so it would be best if you head straight to your dorms to study. This week will determine who stays and who will be sent home. Study hard."

While the remaining student audience uttered disgruntled mumbling as they picked up their trays and headed towards the door, Archer eyed Maya and Sanaya, his expression unreadable.

"You two," he said firmly. "Come with me."

Maya glanced at Sanaya who simply shrugged and picked up her tray while Archer waited. Sanaya did not need to think about what would have happened had Archer not shown up, but she was grateful that ever since she met the man, he seemed to know when she was in trouble and showed up just in time. She placed her tray on the roll away table by the door for students to put their plates, trays and silverware on and waited for Maya to do the same. The two walked side by side as they followed the Guardian who led them from the dining hall through the courtyard into the three story annex building. The almost thirty minute walk in silence was enough to push Sanaya over the edge. She kept sharing glances with Maya, whose big hazel-brown, Bedouin eyes revealed that she too was just as nervous. Sanaya did not want to even speak with Maya telepathically for fear Archer may intercede, so she kept her thoughts to herself.

Once inside the Annex building, where all of the administrative and medical business took place, Archer led them to a small cubicle of a room decorated only with a worn down army green sofa and a desk to which Archer took a seat behind. Maya and Sanaya sat down on the sofa and waited for Archer to speak.

"So, what happened with Elizabeth? From the looks of things, you were ready to knock her head off Sanaya," Archer said, relaxing further into the office and resting both of his palms behind his head.

"She has some serious issues with me Archer," Sanaya explained. "And quite frankly, I'm tired of it. Because of her, almost all of the school hates me and she goes out of her way to make my life more miserable than what it already is."

"I am going to have a talk with her, and then one with her parents," Archer replied flatly. "Arrogant, pretentious pricks they are...that family as a whole has been nothing but trouble for the Academy with the exception of her great grandfather, the famous Van Helsing. The elders know it but refuse to do anything because of Van Helsing's legendary status

Suddenly, it seemed like all of the world's burdens were lifted off of her shoulders, and Sanaya could finally relax. "Thanks Archer..."

"No problem kiddo," he said leaning forward. "You should have told me something sooner. I have been waiting for the opportunity to expel her and-"

"You are going to expel her?" Maya and Sanaya simultaneously gasped.

"I am going to submit a request for her expulsion," Archer admitted. "Now, the elders may not approve. However even a temporary expulsion may do her some good. She isn't as strong as she thinks she is, regardless of her seniority, I have yet to take her out on the field. She just gets away with the 'I'm A Bad Ass' card because of her bloodline and I have been merciful enough not to embarrass her by placing her in a real life fight against vampires. At her rank, I don't think she would fare well against a low grade succubus. The only other reason why she is still here is because she knows everything by the book. However, when the time comes for her to graduate, she may not be selected as a guardian. She will simply be sent home and her family can decide what to do with her."

Sanaya could not believe her ears. She'd always known Elizabeth deep down was scared of her and now she knew why. Maya was right. Elizabeth was indeed jealous of her and found her to be a threat.

"So what are we going to do now?" Sanaya asked after a long moment.

"Well, I brought both of you here to meet someone. Maya, I am sure Sanaya has told you I am taking her on a live hunt tonight. You have proven to be a strong telepath and in time, you will accompany Sanaya on these adventures, but I need for you to work on building physical strength since you have already accomplished mental strength, understand?"

Maya nodded emphatically and took Sanaya's hand and gave her a gentle squeeze.

"In the meantime, both of you will be working with someone very special, and can relate to what you are going through Sanaya. Her name is Eve and she…"

"Is a descendent from the line of Dracula!" Maya gasped. She looked at Sanaya who stared back at her, her eyes wide with confusion.

"I've heard of her…does she really understand what it is we do?" Maya continued.

"Maya!" Sanaya scolded.

"No, it's fine Sanaya. Your friend has every right to be concerned. Now as I was saying- before I was interrupted, Eve has hunted more vampires than I can count. As a matter of fact, Sanaya, she was brought here when she was around your age. The Vatican was going to exterminate her, but it was discovered that she is half human. Before Van Helsing finally killed Dracula, The Count made it his mission to turn all of his living descendants into the undead. Her mother was pregnant with her when she was bitten, and some of the virus was passed down to her, so she was born,not bitten. Her mother, unfortunately, did not survive the birth or the transition. One of the maids who worked for the family rescued her, and delivered her to a nunnery where she was raised until she was sixteen. The head nun brought her here due to an incident involving a priest…"

"What happened to the priest?" Sanaya demanded.

~ 12 ~

Archer chuckled. "Well, the priest thought of himself to be up high enough to try to take advantage of an orphaned girl until he got more than what he bargained for.-She bit him and pretty much drained him. The Vatican then got involved, yada yada yada…and now she has become one of our most effective weapons."

Sanaya swallowed thickly. "So she feeds off of humans and you are pairing us with her because…"

"She cannot pass the virus, so even if she does bite you, you wouldn't turn… But if she were to get pissed off enough and bite, let's say Maya, your friend wouldn't turn. And she does not require blood to sustain herself either. She eats food just like every other human being, but garlic isn't exactly her best friend either."

Sanaya and Maya exchanged uneasy looks.

"Are there more like her?" Maya asked.

"Probably, but not more than likely, half -bloods are rare. The vampire virus is too strong for a fetus to survive the pregnancy. Chances are, Eve was fully developed and days away from coming into the world when her mother was bitten."

"Oh," was all Maya could say as she scanned the tiny room, anxiously anticipating Eve's arrival at any moment.

"Any more questions?" Archer quipped.

When both girls shook their heads, Archer continued. "Good. And while I have your undivided attention Sanaya, it doesn't take a genius to figure out that Maya will be selected as one of your Guardians when the time comes, which is fine, provided she continues to grow and develop her gifts and demonstrate her loyalty to you. But I would like for you to consider Eve. I'm not telling you to. It is your choice, but now is the time to start thinking about it. Four years will go by quickly and…"

"Stop trying to convince the girl who would be best suited for her team," came a thick Hungarian accent from behind the door. Sanaya and Maya turned around to face the enchanting beauty of Eve as she closed the door behind her. She stood just a foot away from where the girls sat, dressed in all black from head to toe: black denim, knee high leather boots; black tank top layered with a black leather coat. The symbol of the cross hung from her neck, while she carried a crossbow in one hand. Thick coils of long, raven hair cascaded down to the center of her back. Eyes the color of the Mediterranean Sea stared back at all three of them from a face as delicate and fair as porcelain. Sanaya could sense Archer's admiration of the Guardian and wondered if the two of them had something going...not that it mattered but still...

"Hello ladies," Eve greeted warmly. "I know Archer has told you everything you need to know about me and it is a pleasure to meet both of you."

Sanaya was the first on her feet with her hand extended. "My name is...""

"Sanaya," Eve finished. "And you are strong. I can feel your energy. The Prophecy has done you no justice."

Sanaya smiled, feeling every bit of proud to be recognized by someone such as Eve.

"And my name is Maya," Maya added, extending her hand as well for Eve to shake.

"Ah, Maya I have heard of you as well...Voodoo roots, no? Use that to your advantage and do not be ashamed of your parentage. We cannot change the conditions under which we are born, but we can use them to our benefit. You will do well when we encounter demons."

"These two will be under your charge throughout the remainder of their stay at The Academy," Archer informed her. "I believe they will benefit the most from your teachings."

"Will I be allowed to take them on live hunts?" Eve asked, turning her attention on to Archer.

"I am taking Sanaya on her first live hunt tonight and I am extending the invitation for you to come along... Maya on the other hand needs a little more sparring and physical conditioning before she will be ready for live combat."

"I can condition her and get her ready. She has to be on the same level as our newest huntress in order to be selected as Guardian."

"Well ladies, I am more than happy to have introduced you both to Eve. If you have any issues, especially when I am not around, she is your go to person. I will text you both her cell for you to immediately save in your contact lists, and with that being said you both are dismissed. Sanaya, I will see you at midnight." Archer redirected his attention to Eve, appearing to be oblivious to the fact Sanaya and Maya had made it out into the hall.

The two walked side by side in companionable silence until they made it into the courtyard before speaking.

"Do you think The Academy will expel Elizabeth?" Maya whispered to Sanaya.

"Shhh, talk to me in my head girl. You know there are students here that can hear a pin drop from a hundred miles away," Sanaya scolded.

"My bad girl..."

But seriously, do you think the school will do it? Maya continued telepathically.

Probably not. Elizabeth is a year away from graduating and if she has been here this long on a reign of terror, I doubt the school will do anything more than a slap on the wrist. Besides, now that I think of it, expelling Elizabeth may cause more problems than do good. Sanaya exhaled sharply. *I think it is a no win situation to be honest.*

I still think that bitch deserves it, Maya huffed mentally. *She's been tormenting new students for as long as I have been here and I have been dying to test my voodoo...*

Don't even go there Maya! We are on hallowed ground and it is bad enough we curse like sailors. But tampering with the dark arts is not going to get you or me anywhere and if you have any hope of becoming a Guardian one day in any capacity, using Voodoo will not cut it, Sanaya thought sharply. *You will get kicked out of this place so fast you won't have time to make your head spin-*

I'm sorry Sanaya! Damn! It was just a thought, Maya huffed.

Well thoughts become actions and that is what Elizabeth wants... Sanaya stopped walking and turned round to face her friend. "Promise me you won't tamper with that stuff Maya," she pleaded after placing her hands on Maya shoulders and forcing her to look at her. "Promise me."

"I promise Sanaya," Maya replied with a groan. "Besides, that stuff scares me anyways...I was just talking."

"Good," was all Sanaya could say before they reached Maya's dormitory.

"Call me as soon as you get in," Maya said with a wide, toothy grin. "I mean it. I don't care if it is four in the morning. I need all of the deets."

"I will. Get some rest." Sanaya gave Maya a quick hug before the two separated and Sanaya continued her stroll to her dorm which was another twenty minutes away. She thought about her best friend and her Creole roots and wondered if it was just in her blood to answer the call of the dark realms. Her mother was of Haitian and Spanish descent and her father was a regular Caucasian man who became enchanted by the spell of a Voodoo priestess seeking a sperm donor, which is where

~ 16 ~

Maya got her exotic look from. Large, oval shaped eyes, lined with the thickest and longest natural eye lashes that would make Maybelline products jealous, butter cream skin as smooth as silk, a shapely body compared to Sanaya's tall, thin frame; it was of pure wonder why Maya wasn't the bell of the school. But then again, no, it wasn't because it all boiled down to Elizabeth.

Sanaya continued her stroll, bypassing a few other students who eyed her with quiet curiosity but none dared to approach. When she made it to her building, she used hyper speed to dodge some of the senior members of the student body that hung around in the lobby. She didn't stop until she was up the two flights of stairs and locked away in the privacy of her room. She kicked off of her shoes, climbed onto her bed and cut on the small flat screen Archer had snuck in for her to zone out for the next few hours before it was time for her to go out on her first hunt. Five minutes into The Real House Wives of Atlanta, she was out like a light, and her last fleeting thought was her hoping to wake up in time due to her lack of mental strength to set the alarm on her phone for midnight. Archer would just have to understand.

CHAPTER THREE

Surprisingly Sanaya awoke just twenty minutes before midnight. She dashed to her closet, pulled out a pair of her black and white Juicy sweats with the matching hoodie, pulled back her shoulder length hair into a bun, jammed her feet into her Nikes, grabbed her keys, and raced to the courtyard where Archer was waiting. He stood idly underneath her favorite tree sporting a long trench coat, black leather pants, and steel toed boots. His auburn hair was no longer in the casual trim which kept his hair just above his ears; now, it was freshly shaved in a buzz cut, giving him a more rugged appearance. Off to his right she detected the presence of Eve and made it a point to acknowledge her to let them both know she was ready.

"Very good. You sensed me," Eve grinned emerging from the shadows. "Had you not, I would have been concerned."

"I think I have been sensing vampires all of my life," Sanaya said quietly, instantly grabbing Archer's attention. "But, I didn't know that I was until I came here and now it is easy for me to identify."

"I understand," Eve said offering her a reassuring smile.

" Now we begin," Archer stated coolly. "First thing's first though,every huntress must choose her weapon." He opened his trench coat revealing a series of weapons for her to choose from. "Upon graduation, there will be a ceremony in which you will be handed a very special weapon that has been used since the first huntress came into existence.Until then, pick one to use for tonight."

Sanaya studied the options before her. She was pretty handy with a short blade, she wasn't into the nun chucks,throwing stars-not even.Her eyes drifted to the silver tipped arrows and wondered where the rest of the weapon was.

"Eve has the bow in case you were wondering. You will have the opportunity to use it, however, the bow and arrow and the cross bow are better for long range combat. Tonight, you are going hand to hand." Archer said as he reached into the trench and pulled out a wooden stake with a silver tip. "Here, this is what you will use tonight. We are going vampire hunting darling."

Sanaya accepted the stake and gently raked her finger across the pointed silver tip. She appreciated its light density and wondered how many times the priests dunked this weapon in holy water to ensure its effectiveness.

"This stake is yours for the taking my dear," Archer continued. "Made from Lebanese Cedar, which is supposed to contain its own natural spiritual properties, this is probably the most effective weapon in killing vamps.Hell, you can throw werewolves into the mix too because of the silver. Pierce the heart of a blood sucker, the bastard goes straight to ash upon contact."

Sanaya felt herself tightening her grip on the weapon.

"Next, you have already experienced a run in with a vampire, your own father. So you know how strong they are, and how fast they move. As a matter of fact, huntress, you have in your possession the same abilities as vampires: heightened senses to sight, sound, touch, taste and smell. You can detect them just as they can detect their prey. You already know you have the ability to move in hyper speed but what you didn't know is that I have clocked you going from zero to almost ninety miles in less than two seconds which is absolutely amazing. It makes me wonder what you will be able to do as a fully matured huntress." Archer paused to give her some time to let the information sink in. Eve crossed her arms and leaned against the Willow and waited for him to resume.

"Also," he continued, "you are immune to all vampire and werewolf bites along with the negative forces that come from the Organization of Darkness…and most human diseases. However, that doesn't mean you are invincible." He gives Sanaya a hard look. "You can still be killed like any other human caught in a car accident or the unsuspecting gunshot victim. In your body, not only do you have red and white blood cells, you have a shit load of natural silver that is pumped within you so if you ever find yourself separated from me or Eve and the fucker is quick enough to successfully bite you, your blood will incinerate it before your blood hits the back of its throat. And just in case we do get separated, I don't know if you realize this or not, but when you were brought here unconscious, members of the Vatican tattooed you on the back of your neck, right at the tip of your spine and between your shoulders. That symbol is our own personal GPS system and I will be able to find you anywhere in the world. Typically, the symbol is tattooed at birth, but some unfortunate things happened and we don't have all night for me to explain. Just know that we will be with you and you can trust that we will have your back."

Archer paused, allowing her time for the information to sink in. Eve checked her watch and tapped her foot anxiously as she leaned against the tree.

"Vatican City was built on hallowed and blessed ground which ultimately makes it the safest place on the planet. Evil cannot cross over the heavily prayed over threshold, which means we have to go outside of the city…Tonight, we are hitting the very busy streets of Rome." And with that, Archer led the two of them from the courtyard to the parking lot where his black 2016 Maserati awaited them.

"You ladies should consider yourselves lucky," Archer said jokingly as he *chirped, chirped* the unlocking mechanism to the expensive car. "Only the select few are fortunate enough to ride in the bat mobile."

As Eve reached for the handle of the front passenger door, Archer beat her to the punch and opened the door for her with a grin. She offered a shy smile and got in without a word.

"And only the best get to ride shot gun." He added with a wink to Sanaya.

Sanaya simply shook her head and slid into the backseat. Archer must have been in a rare moment because it was not often he displayed such playfulness. Normally, he was all no nonsense and straight business, but Sanaya assumed his obvious attraction to Eve had something to do with it.

The smooth jet black leathery interior was a dream and Sanaya pictured herself speeding off into the night in a car just like Archer's Maserati. Fully loaded with automatic seat warmers, GPS monitoring, cruise control and the ability to shift gears to accelerate to a speed of 185 mph, Sanaya believed his car to be a vampire hunter's dream. As Archer smoothly set the car in reverse and back out of the parking lot, she closed her eyes and stuck her head out of the window and welcomed the chill of the cool night air to brush against her face. Tonight, she would learn what it meant to be a huntress and she could not think of any better way to step into her destiny.

■■■

Meanwhile...

High above in a Manhattan tower overlooking the city, three entities masking themselves as prominent businessmen dressed in suits met in a boardroom. Sterile white walls stretched across the large meeting room before coming to an end where the clear glass windows provided a spectacular view of night sky and the city below illuminated with the contrasting neon colors along with the overall electric aura that surrounded the city. Manhattan for the last twenty or so years had not only been primary feeding grounds for the Organization of Darkness, but it's ideal location for headquarters. The main office was in Washington, D.C. where all of the devil's work was conducted above ground, but here in Manhattan was where just about every master vampire established his lair.

There was something undefinable about the state of New York. The humans were just as gritty, just as corrupt; filled with lies and greed like fattened sheep. And just like the wolves, the vampires swarmed in on the unsuspecting humans, gorging themselves in blood and living the lives of modern day gods. And for the lucky victims who were unfortunate to meet their end through the bite of a Master level vampire, were offered a choice: to live in leisure and pleasure for however long they existed in this earth realm as an immortal with the thirst for blood, or to die honorably with the hope that their choice permitted them entrance into heaven's gates.

Petronius, the oldest of the three sat at the head of the table with his legs crossed, his hands forming a tent and his lap top open, exposing a particular webpage he left open for his colleague's review. Dressed in a dark three piece Armani exclusive, the ancient vampire's eyes met the curious stares of fellow masters, and cleared his throat before speaking.

"I called this meeting betwixt the three of us tonight because I have just received word that The Huntress is out on her first hunt…" He allowed the statement to hang in the air as the two younger vampires allowed the information to sink in.

"For seventeen years we searched for her," came the sallow, wheezy voice of Alex, a former protégé of Petronius. He was the only vampire at the table to survive an attack from a Guardian using a blessed blade, and as a result his windpipe was no longer functioning as he took in labored breaths. Regardless of how much he fed, nothing seemed to heal the wound, but somehow he survived.

"Indeed we did," Petronius added, his pale green eyes illuminating a soft neon glow.

"We even managed to locate and turn her own father and-"

"He was killed by a Guardian and she got away," Daemon interrupted.

Petronius directed his gaze on the master vampire with the scar that ran down his face from his temple to his jawline. Daemon's eyes illuminated a deep crimson but dared not openly challenge Petronius, at least not yet. Petronius took note of the subtle threat but maintained his focus on the task at hand: finding the slayer.

"Our spies have indicated that she is on Guardian land but tonight she is outside of the protective barrier," Petronius continued.

"We have four years until she matures," Alex added with a wheeze.

"We should send out everything we have now while she is young. We missed the opportunity once and it would be foolish if we miss it again," Daemon replied with a scowl.

"Ah, but there is something you are missing Daemon. Instead of always being quick to use brute force, a much more shrewd and intellectual approach in times like these is needed," Petronius coolly replied.

"And what is that?"

"You two are not old enough to understand why it has been two thousand years since the last slayer walked this earth…" Petronius began as he uncrossed his legs and faced forward, holding both vampires' attention. "All slayers are born female, which is a fatal weakness that our side of the horizon craves to exploit. Two thousand years ago, it was discovered by our kind that once every few years, her body's resistance to our bite is lowered. She goes through a period of needing when she ovulates followed by the normal female menstrual cycle that flushes her system. During that time she will hunt less and fall under heavy guard by her guardians because she is weaker and unable to resist our…charms." Petronius swallowed thickly before continuing. "Her scent during that time is intoxicating.So much so, that it will make you want to risk daylight just to get to her-"

"Tell us what happened two thousand years ago!" Alex demanded licking his own lips as his fangs crested.

~ 23 ~

"Patience my friend," Petronius said fighting back a shudder that threatened to undo his cool façade. "Two thousand years ago, the huntress of that time actually fell in love with one of our own. She had forsaken her vow to the Vatican, to the Light, to her Guardians for a *vampire* which resulted in a pregnancy."

The two other vampires hissed.

"You lie!" Daemon exclaimed.

"Do I?" Petronius challenged. "Smell me my brother, do I carry the scent of deceit?" He didn't wait for Daemon to respond when he continued. "She carried his seed until the very end of the pregnancy until her guardians had found her, hidden in the deserts of the Fertile Crescent where she'd given birth to the very first day walker. The Guardians, heartbroken but committed to their mission, not only killed the infant believing it to be an abomination, but retrieved the slayer, holding her hostage behind the protective walls of the First Church until she died an old, broken woman. The vampire that impregnated her was killed by one of the guardians not soon after…but, think of it… we have another opportunity to appease the beast and create another day walker, one whose bite may change history and the future of all vampires."

"And he would become the most powerful of us all and may decide to hold the gift unto himself and deliver it to those who decide to follow him," Daemon scoffed. "I say kill her and be done with it."

"No, we will groom him to our ways and our goals," Petronius replied with a grin.

"And what of the Slayer? She may refuse us access to her child. You know how human women are about their young…" Alex quizzed.

"A problem that can be remedied easily," Petronius said dismissively. "We kill her as soon as the child is pulled from her womb."

Petronius eased back into the office chair and allowed the plan to marinate deep into his colleague's psyches. This would indeed please The Beast and position them into a seat of more power.

"And which vampire will we send on this dangerous mission? How will he infiltrate The Academy?" Daemon asked, appearing to be suddenly interested in the plan.

"For now, we will not send a vampire. That is obviously impossible. A seduction of this magnitude takes time and I am willing to invest four years before going in for the kill. We will send a compromised potential guardian, a 'bad boy' to entice her."

"And just where the hell are we going to find a potential yet compromised guardian?" Daemon stood up impatiently and began pacing the room.

"Relax Daemon. I have already considered who it will be. There is a young man with various powerful gifts awaiting trial in a juvenile court. My workers, varying demons and succubae have been working on his family for generations, courtesy of a very sinful ancestor and now his future is bleak. He is our mole and doesn't even know it yet. One of my workers has already sent word to retrieve this young potential to try to reverse his fate. Not only is he angry, but he is gifted and used his abilities for selfish purposes. He is handsome, charming and street smart...the perfect recipe for a teenaged heartbreak."

"And you are certain he will be the key to her undoing?" Daemon questioned skeptically.

"Beyond...he has a darkness within him that is enough to eclipse the sun and had I not considered him for this specific purpose, I would have turned him myself. He will do our empire good."

"And if he is successful, she may choose him as one of her Guardians." Alex added with a cough.

"At midnight on her twenty first birthday, I believe he has the capability…" Petronius stood up from his seat and walked over to the window, looking down on the city below.

"When will she go into her needing?" Daemon asked, his fangs fully extended, desire wafting from his pores.

"As soon as she turns twenty one. From there, there is a seven day window. I plan to turn him immediately after her coronation as the slayer. In three days, he will return to her and they will reunite as lovers do."

"And what if his seed doesn't take?" Alex inquired with concern.

"That is a risk I am willing to take." Petronius turned away from the view and faced his fellow conspirators. "Gentlemen, our meeting is adjourned. The sun will rise soon which means it is time for us to retire to our lairs. We will reconvene on the next full moon to discuss things in detail. Four years is not that far away."

"Indeed it is not," Alex added, licking his lips and trembling with desire. "I would love to be the one to service her during her needing."

"And she would stake you on sight my friend," Petronius chuckled. "All of us would love to be the one to service her during that period, but unfortunately, there is something much bigger at stake than idle pleasures of the flesh. Until the next moon. Feed well." Petronius dematerialized in puff of mist and disappeared into the night.

Alex bid Daemon farewell with a nod before converting into mist, leaving the scarred vampire alone with his thoughts.

"Farewell Petronius," he muttered to himself as he deconstructed into the airwaves. "Farewell indeed."

CHAPTER FOUR

Sanaya gripped the silver stake tightly behind her back as she faced off with her first vampire target. Archer literally dropped her off just outside of the back alley behind one of the popular Italian clubs which happened to be a popular vampire feeding ground. She could still hear the blaring pop music vibrating through the streets of Rome, as she studied the creature before her. The moment he pulled off, her skin began to tingle and prickle and all of her senses heightened. Fear was no longer an issue. She detected the presence of two more hiding off in the shadows and every muscle in her body twitched with tension. She narrowed her gaze at the creature. Red, glowing eyes glared back at her. Fangs fully extended and still dripping with the blood of the victim it had been feeding on. Scraggly blonde hair, tanned skin,which indicated that this is a recent turn,ripped denim and a blood soaked blue crew neck. Standing at about 5'8"…oh yeah, Sanaya could take her.

The vampire hissed before transforming into vapor and Sanaya forced herself to become still like a living, breathing statue. She waited for the precise moment when the vampire would materialize out of the vapor and then she became liquid motion. From her training, she knew baby vampires were impulsive and blinded by their all-consuming thirst for blood. She landed a strong kick to the entity's jaw while she hit the ground smoothly. The vampire stumbled back and lunged for her again, this time joined by the two other vampires that were hiding in the shadows. Sanaya sensed them before they could land a punch, and once again, she became a blur. Using her hyper speed, she launched a series of hard kicks and punches, more enraged by the minute. She pictured the countless innocents whose loved ones were taken from them because of these vermin. She remembered her own loss and for that, these bastards would pay. One of them, a tall, lanky young man who appeared to be in his early twenties was lucky enough to knock her off balance. She hit the concrete with a hard thud landing on her shoulder and dislocating it in the process. She howled in pain but that would not stop her.

She could hear the quickened footsteps and the familiar presence of Archer and Eve running to her aid, but she didn't need them. She was on her feet instantly, adrenaline burning away the pain.Clutching the silver tipped stake, she took aim and flung it in the center of the tall, lanky vampire's chest, incinerating him instantly. Eve appeared out of the nothingness and was on the blonde vampire, decapitating her with her blade while Archer brought down the other, a short red head, with a silver tipped arrow using the cross bow. With adrenaline still flooding her nervous system, Sanaya reared her head back and released a war cry, her voice echoing in the alley. Despite her shoulder being dislocated, her internal vampire tracking system was still on high alert and it sent her running down the alley at top speed. She heard Archer and Eve call out her name, but she could not bring herself to turn around. No, she would not be deterred!

She became one with the night, feeling strengthened by its seductive call to hunt those who hide underneath its protective covering. A howl could be heard off in the distance when she came to a stop just outside of a local bar two miles south from the club. Gooseflesh blanketed her brown skin and the overall feeling of dread caused knots to form in her stomach forcing her to double over with nausea. She could hear Eve in her mind begging her to fall back, but her naturally stubborn nature refused to answer. This particular street seemed to be a dead zone.No human stragglers in sight, not even the drunken fools who did not know their limit and had to be escorted out by the guards; no sound other than her own labored breaths could be heard for what seemed like miles. The feeling of dread intensified, bringing her to her knees and she finally sent Archer a mental SOS. Her instincts told her to get up and run when her mind felt the gentle caress of an intruder attempting a telepathic lock. She mentally sealed herself in, but the force was too strong and pried her mind open like a soda can.

And what brings a young beauty like yourself into my side of town? The deep baritone voice of something male whispered in Italian in her mind.

Before she could respond, someone grabbed her from behind and hoisted her on his shoulder and the next thing she knew they were on the move. She heard Eve shouting something. However, her mind was elsewhere, trying to understand what just happened. The connection to the entity remained until Archer tossed her in the backseat of his Maserati with him having to strap her in himself.

Instant yearning for the stranger in her mind brought tears to her eyes. She had to get to that voice!

She struggled to break free from the seat belt when Eve crawled in next to her and held her wrists firmly against her thighs.

"Listen to me Sanaya," She said firmly. Her midnight blue eyes boring into her; her own fangs now fully extended. "You have been called.I need you to breathe."

Archer quickly started the engine. "This is my fault. I should have never brought her out! It is too soon!"

"Breath Sanaya," Eve continued.

Sanaya slowly began to relax as she focused on Eve and mimicked her breathing. In the meantime, Archer drove like a madman on mission, pushing the Maserati to maximum speed as they drove through the countryside in the opposite direction of the Vatican.

"Where are you going?" Eve panicked, releasing Sanaya's wrists and looking behind them.

"Can't take her back immediately. We are being trailed. I'm sure you know what that was that called her. How the fuck did we not know that a *master* vampire was in our midst?" With one hand on the steering wheel he yanked his phone out from his side pocket and hit dial.

"He must've been a recent elevation because as much as I have been out in the field, I hadn't detected his presence either. Who are you calling?"

"The Vatican. This is serious and so close to the Academy? What if that had been one of our other senior students Eve? Huh?" There was a pause and Eve didn't bother to respond due to someone obviously answering the phone.

"Hey Tia this is Archer and we have a very serious problem...no...she was called by a fuckin' master level vampire while out in the field...uh huh...I am sending you our location and which direction we are headed in now...yes a full guardian escort is needed. Roger that." He disconnected the call and glanced into the rearview mirror at Sanaya. "How is our Slayer?"

"A little dazed but I think she is coming around," Eve said giving Sanaya's hand a gentle squeeze. "I think the connection is severed because she is no longer trying to make a bolt for it."

They drove at Mach speed for another twenty minutes before slowly coming to a halt in front of a small church just a few miles away from a cliff overlooking the ocean. Sanaya continued to gaze out of the window, hypnotized by the scenery of a clear night sky blanketing mile after mile of fields of green. She no longer felt the seductive caress intermingling with the overwhelming sense of dread and the urge to run into death's embrace head on. She relaxed, leaned her head against the leathery backseat and allowed Archer to drive them away to safety.

The sun still had yet to rise, but she could sense its warm, life giving rays off in the distance. Her phone began to vibrate on her hip and she knew it was Maya dying to know the scoop. She could feel Eve studying her as she pulled out her phone to decline the call but follow up with a text message.

Call u later. Not home yet.

She slid the phone back into her pocket and returned her gaze to the scenery, enchanted by the sweeping slopes of the hills in the countryside; the miles upon miles of vineyards; and the overall beauty of the landscape. When they finally came to a stop in front of the church, Archer was the first out of the car with his Berretta drawn. Eve slid out using the driver passenger's side door and both of them were at Sanaya's side when she reached for the handle to push the door open. Archer led them up the stoned pathway through the iron gate and knocked patiently on the wooden door decorated with a gold cross. The church sat on a single story surrounded by shrubbery and a small garden patch that lined the walkway. When the aging priest finally answered the door, he simply nodded at Archer allowing him to pass. When Eve went to approach him, he motioned the sign of the cross over his chest and stepped to the side, careful to put as much distance between them as possible. But with Sanaya, he fell to his knees and lowered his head to the ground uttering praises. Sanaya gave Archer a pleading look and he immediately helped the priest to his feet.

"Bless you child!" He continued to utter, his blue eyes red with shed tears. "We have something to continue to fight for…to believe in."

As a warm gesture, Archer dusted off the priest's red robing but the cleric politely ushered him away. The priest beckoned for them to follow him, bypassing row after row of pews followed by the alter where the man of cloth would feed the spirits of his parishioners with a word from God, into a back room that provided a twin bed, a dresser and gated window.

"She can rest here," the cleric offered with a thick Italian accent. "I have other rooms for the both of you to rest until the other Guardians arrive,but I do not understand the need when daylight is near."

"There are other entities that are not banished to the darkness, Father Lorenzo," Archer stated calmly.

The priest nodded as Sanaya took a seat on the twin bed.

"Rest here kid. The team should be here shortly and I know you need a moment to gather your thoughts and whatnot…"

Archer waited for Father Lorenzo to escort Eve down the hall to another room before continuing. Sanaya figured she was about to receive an earful for taking off on her own like she did and anxiously awaited the verbal chastising she clearly deserved,but when their eyes met, pride shone in his, something she did not expect.

"Good job kid," he said finally after a beat. "I mean it. The fact that you were willing to take on three vampires on your own, dislocating your shoulder in the process,which by the way still needs to be looked at, and then you hone in on a master level vampire's lair smack dab in the middle of Rome." He rubbed the back of his neck. "Bad ass."

"Thanks Archer," was all she could say.

"No need to thank me. I should be thanking you. I have several scheduled field tests with some of your peers, and none of us had even caught on to the fact that there is a master in our midst which could lead to some serious consequences…damn girl, if you are this strong at seventeen it makes me wonder what you are going to be like at twenty one." He paused before continuing. "I will have Eve come and pop your shoulder back into place."

At the mere mention of her shoulder, pain immediately shot up her arm causing her to groan.

"I'll go get Eve." Archer turned around and left while Sanaya fell back on the twin bed. As another wave a pain coursed through her, off in the distance, she could hear the faint voice of the vampire in her mind calling her. She blocked him out, finally and closed her eyes trying to focus on anything else other than the pain. Rolling onto her side, she inhaled deeply and prayed that the guardian team that was supposed to come arrived soon, as that same feeling of dread crept back into her system.

Yeah, they needed to get here stat.

CHAPTER FIVE

The Guardians arrived not even thirty minutes after Eve came into the room and popped her shoulder back into place. The sun had just begun to peak over the horizon, and Sanaya struggled to keep her eyes open. Her body's sluggish movements were enough to plead her case in missing classes today, but then again the last thing she wanted to do was spend most of her day alone and trapped in her room. Each of the Guardians had regarded her with a level of high respect, and upon leaving the church, they surrounded her in the traditional guardian formation: two at her front, two at her sides, and two at her back with Eve and Archer guarding the flank. Archer held the door to his Maserati open for her, as she climbed in the back. Eve made it a point to nestle in next to her on the other side.

Every bone in her body ached, and as they drove in a caravan on their way back to the Academy, Eve suggested that she soak in the tub with some bath salts she would provide for her and catching an hour or two of sleep before making it to at least one of her classes. Class began at seven. Sanaya checked her watch and it was already nearing 6:30. She would definitely miss her English Lit class and her World Studies class. She may make it to The Dimensions of Hell 101 and now that she was no longer allowed to spar with her peers, her Weapons and Physical Fitness class left two hours of free time, unless Archer told her otherwise. So, she figured that could be used for more sleep and recovery.

Her eye balls felt like she dipped them and rolled them in sand before placing them back into her sockets, and her body still hummed with the feeling of dread. She caught Eve staring at her and shifted uneasily in her seat. Eve knew the connection wasn't totally broken.

"Are you alright?" She asked with her Romanian accent thicker than usual.

"Yeah, yeah…I'm good," Sanaya replied quickly trying not to broach the subject with Archer in the vicinity. She managed to successfully block him from reading her, but the effort had been draining and causing more fatigue than what she could fight against.

"No, you are not. You forget you are speaking to a vampire," she whispered, understanding Sanaya's discomfort with giving Archer all of the details.

"I don't think you should go out in the field again until we put the vampire down," Eve continued.

"I can hear you two you know," Archer frowned. "And she won't. Too dangerous. The instant she steps outside of The Academy, he will call her. They already have a mind lock."

"But-" Sanaya started to argue but was instantly cut off by Archer's hard stare from the rearview mirror.

"No. End. Of. Discussion. And I am cancelling all scheduled field tests until further notice. You will spar with experienced Guardians until then."

Sanaya exhaled sharply and slumped back into her seat. She was huntress for crying out loud! This was her destiny and what she was being trained to do. She should be the one to hunt the master vampire and put him out of his misery.

"We will talk more later," Eve whispered gently patting her hand.

Sanaya simply nodded. What else was there for them to talk about?

"Oh and one more thing Sanaya," Archer declared firmly, his eyes still focused on the road.

"Yes?"

"Until this master is put down for good, you will be under twenty four hour guard beginning the moment your foot touches the pavement at The Academy. I would explain to you the necessity of such extreme precautions but I take it you would rather hear it from Eve."

Sanaya's eyes widened as she glanced at Eve who looked away quickly. So it was going to be *that* kind of conversation best explained by another female. Great. They drove the rest of the way in silence and as soon as Archer pulled into the parking lot, she was once again surrounded by the team of Guardians.

Great...even better. Now the whole school is going to think I am under some special privilege just for being born, she thought to herself. *Fuck my life.*

Just as Sanaya predicted, students and senior staff stopped in their tracks to observe the obvious parade of Guardians escorting her to her room. She cringed as she felt the curious, and the few hateful stares of her peers; her stomach did backflips as she listened in on the whispers and private thoughts that revealed some of the onlookers true feelings.

Who does she think she is?

What did the freak do this time?

Attention whore!

Full Guardian escort? Does that mean it is time?

I don't see what the big deal is...she isn't special...

Sanaya lowered her head and tried to tune out the myriad of thoughts, feeling like she was being mentally and emotionally stoned. When she finally made it to her room, she requested-better yet-demanded at least five minutes of privacy with Eve swearing to her that she would return so they could talk. Of course, she knew she would only be granted privacy within the space of her room. At least three Guardians were outside of her door keeping watch. Tossing her hoodie on her messy

~ 36 ~

bed, she went straight for the tiny compartment of a shower and cut the water on as hot as she could physically stand it. She checked her phone once again, not expecting any other calls or messages from anyone other than Maya, and just as she expected, word must have traveled fast because Maya's number popped up on the screen as soon as she unlocked her phone.

Sanaya inhaled deeply before answering. "Yeah?"

"Uh weren't you supposed to call me?" Maya snapped, her normally calm voice climbing a few notches higher.

"I just got in Maya, like literally." Sanaya collapsed on the bed and closed her eyes.

"Well, apparently your entrance caused a big stir. Full Guardian escort? What the hell happened Sanaya?"

"It's a long story-"

"I don't want to hear that crap," Maya quipped. "Spill it."

"Did you sleep at all last night?" Sanaya asked with a chuckle.

"Hell no! I was up all night worrying about you." Maya's tone suddenly shifted from agitated to concerned. "What happened?"

Sanaya quickly gave her friend a quick rundown of the night's events, and when she touched on the subject of the master vampire, Maya's gasp felt like it sucked what little life she had in her, out of her.

"You mind locked with a *master* vampire? Do you know how dangerous that is? He could trail you for the rest of your life until someone puts him down-"

"So that explains the presidential entourage," Sanaya released a sigh.

"Yeah, and that means that the school is going to be locked down for a while..." Maya paused before speaking. "Are you alright?"

"Oh now you asked," Sanaya teased, but quickly changed her tone when Maya didn't laugh. "I guess I'm alright. I am exhausted though."

"Not coming to class?"

"Nah...Archer said he will waive the first two so I can get some rest."

"Ok, well I will give you my notes,and Sanaya?"

"Huh?"

"How did it feel to actually kill one those fuckers?"

Sanaya smiled and paused as she thought about it. "Good...it felt good."

She could almost hear Maya smiling. "Good. You know Elizabeth is going to turn green with hate."

"As long as she doesn't try me like she did last night, I don't care what color she turns."

Maya snickered. "Well, cool I guess I will see you later?"

Sanaya yawned. "Yup. You know the drill. Text me later YaYa."

"Alright 'naya."

The two disconnected and Sanaya jumped up and went straight to the shower. She hoped that whatever Eve had to discuss with her was done quickly, because her entire body felt like she'd been used as a punching bag and then dumped off of a cliff.

CHAPTER SIX

Sanaya felt the suffocating weight of darkness wash over her, triggering every natural fighting instinct she possessed into overdrive. Running as fast as her legs could carry her, she suddenly felt sluggish, as if her ankles had become anvils, nearly succumbing to the burn travelling from her calf muscles all the way up to her thighs. She sucked in another deep breath and felt the sting of the icy air penetrate her lungs. Coughing, stumbling, and blind in the absolute darkness, she flinched as a she felt the gentle and all too personal caress of invisible hands run down her spine. She stopped to focus her senses on the possible threat that lurked in the pitch blackness which surrounded her. Patting her left pocket for her small bowie knife, she cursed when she realized it was not in her possession.

"Damn it!"

Another gentle caress brushed against her rear end and she spun around to face the offender. When she found no one she turned around again.

"My you are a delicacy," came the deep velvety baritone and eerily seductive voice from the nothingness. "Not what I expected."

"Who are you?!" She demanded, struggling to keep her tone calm and even. "What do you want?"

"The question is not what I want. Although…"

A warm hand ran down her exposed arm, sending gentle ripples of pleasure into her system. She gasped and wiped away a bead of sweat. "DO NOT TOUCH ME!"

The voice chuckled, indicating to her that the entity had to be at least two feet to her right. She spun around, hoping to face off with the intruder.

"The question has always been…what do you want? Slayer…"

"I promise you," Sanaya seethed, tightening her fists. "I will cut out your heart and watch you burn in the sunlight!"

"We shall see about that," the voice challenged. "But there are other things I would prefer doing."

Suddenly she was naked and she covered herself as best she could, trembling at the knowledge of what potentially could happen next.

"Ah..." The entity inhaled deeply. "You smell absolutely intoxicating...come to me slayer..."

"No," Sanaya whimpered as her body is flooded with pleasure. "No, don't do this..."

"Come to me," the voice demanded. "I cannot have you like this."

"Sanaya... Sanaya..." Sanaya raised her head in the darkness listening to the urgent call of her name and realized she had been asleep.

"Sanaya! Sanaya wake up!"

"No! Come to me tonight Slayer! Come to-"

Sanaya shot up in her bed, breathing heavily and soaked with sweat. Eve jumped back to give her some space as Maya looked down on her friend with concern. Wiping her face, she pushed her hair back and leaned against the headboard and waited for her vision to focus.

"Sanaya are you alright?" Eve questioned. Her blue eyes wide with worry and her crossbow fully loaded at her hip.

"How long have I been out?" Sanaya asked clearing her throat.

"I called you like a million times, " Maya said marching closer to the bed. "You wouldn't answer. Eve tried calling you, and even tried knocking on the door. When you still didn't answer, she went to get the master key from Archer and-"

Eve placed her cool hand on Sanaya's forehead, feeling for her temperature. "You are burning up."

~ 40 ~

She then, stepped away and ran outside of the room where Sanaya sensed Archer awaiting. Sanaya groaned.

"Like for real girl, are you good?" Maya asked taking a seat at the edge of the bed.

"I don't know Maya. I think that master is going to try to come for me, but the scary part is: I don't think I can fight him."

Eve and Maya exchanged worried looks, with Eve returning her attention to Sanaya.

"He is attempting a seduction," Eve stated evenly. "He cannot breach campus grounds so he is trying to draw you to him."

"What am I going to do? Is he going to like…haunt me in my dreams?" Sanaya asked covering her face with her hands.

"Yes. But I know something that can remedy that until he is killed." Eve began to pace. "Thank God for the sun… we have some time to put together something." She stopped pacing to reply to the text notification buzz that went off. "I have to go. I will be back in an hour when the sun sets. You two stick together." Eve nodded at Maya who stared at her best friend, worry written all over her pretty face. "And you Maya…keep an eye on Sanaya. She is going to feel things her body is not ready to handle and even though she will be under heavy guard, you might be the only one capable of talking some sense into her."

Maya nodded as Eve hurriedly rushed out of the door.

Walking to the cafeteria with three highly armed Guardians would have been a nightmare had it not been for Maya distracting her from the curious glances, and gossipy whispers of their peers. Sanaya spotted Elizabeth in her usual spot; seated smack dab in the middle of the dining hall surrounded by her mindless groupies and her goofball boyfriend, Brent. Sanaya smiled in her direction when their eyes met, fury blazing in Van Helsing's descendant's emerald green eyes. Sanaya chuckled as she grabbed a plate, nudging Maya to glance at the table where Elizabeth sat to witness the collective glares from the group of the Academy's most popular students.

"Girl she is pissed off," Maya snickered piling her plate with Spaghetti.

"I know. She is so mad the strands of her hair are levitating," Sanaya whispered.

The three Guardians that escorted them, hung back near the entrance and exit doors, surveying the room.

The two located a table several feet away from where Elizabeth sat, completely disregarding her hard stare.

"I think there is something mentally wrong with her," Sanaya quipped, taking in a mouthful of spaghetti. "She will not quit staring."

They ate in companionable silence, Sanaya lost in her thoughts of last night's action and the end result. The memory of her father coming home as the entity she was destined to hunt darkened her mood. Since her arrival to The Academy, she had not grieved much for either of her parents. Neither of her parents acted like they even wanted to be parents for as long as she could remember. Of course there were glimpses of Patrice acting like a mother, but those moments came far and few between. It was more of an obligation, on Patrice's part and an inconvenience for Roland. But still, her heart ached at the fact that she did not possess the same luxury other students had: a home to return to during the summer and winter months to celebrate mile stones and holidays. What sobered her reality was the fact that Maya sat across from her and as far as she knew, Yaya is her family.

As she scraped the last of her spaghetti into her mouth, she sensed the presence of someone new enter the building, flanked by two more Guardians. She turned around to see who the new guy happened to be, and the instant her eyes laid on him, there seemed to be a rippling effect in the room. The kid had to be almost six feet tall, his black ripped shirt exposing multiple tattoos trailing the hardened biceps on the even dark tanned skin that called out to every female in the room to touch. Dark eyes scanned the room with scrutiny before concentrating on the task at hand: grabbing a plate. Full lips to match with a broad nose and straight black hair cut to a short carefully gelled hair style indicating his rebellious nature and the competing racial duality which added to his already attractive allure. Sanaya glanced at Maya, who was clearly in the same trance as every other female in the room.

Who is that? Maya mentally drooled, still staring at the obvious new kid on the block.

I don't know… Sanaya turned to steal a quick look in his direction. *But that is six feet of fineness and pure trouble.*

I don't mind trouble… Maya gushed. *Where the hell did the Vatican find him?*

Sanaya shrugged. *I don't know, but look check it out.* She tilted her head in Elizabeth's direction. *We aren't the only ones who caught his attention. Betcha ten bucks Elizabeth is going to swoop in like a vulture and sink her talons in him.*

Maya rolled her eyes. *Which means Bradley is about to be on the outskirts…*

Yup… The sad reality made Sanaya turn around and finish her meal, with Maya simply picking at what was left of her meatballs.

Soon, a sudden shift in the atmosphere made Sanaya look up once again, when she felt the presence of the handsome stranger approaching her from behind. Seeing him up close made her heart flutter and she could sense Maya on the brink of going into a cardiac arrest. A familiar Guardian, a seer specializing in past and future events, plus a specially trained martial artist, stood next to him with her arms folded and a slight grin. She already knew what was up.

"Excuse me," the stranger began politely. His voice alone sent chills down Sanaya's spine. "Can I sit here? Every table is full and-"

"Yeah, sure…" Sanaya stammered, clearing her throat. "Go ahead."

"Cool." He took a seat next to her, accidently brushing her arm with his. "My bad…my name is Trent." He extended his hand for her to shake which she nervously accepted.

God his hand is warm, she thought to herself. She could hear Maya mentally shrieking in excitement. "My name is Sanaya, and this is my best friend Maya."

He reached across the table to shake Maya's hand before relaxing in his seat.

"Dinner will end in about twenty minutes," Tia interjected checking her watch. "So make it quick. We still have to get you settled in. I will be outside." The Guardian disappeared quickly through the double doors leaving the trio alone at the table.

"How did you end up here?" Maya wasted no time when trying to get to know someone, and for once Sanaya was grateful for her assertiveness.

"Well," Trent began after taking a bite of his garlic bread. "I was in the system for a while…"

"Foster system?" Maya pressed.

"Yeah, that and juvie. Nobody gets me and never did…I saw shit nobody else saw, fought back and then got into some trouble behind it." He took another bite. "Anyways, I was facing time for a crime I didn't commit when the guardians came and schooled me on what I am. They did something to wrangle me out of the juvie system and brought me from the states here."

"Well, welcome!" Maya chirped.

"Thanks," Trent replied with gratitude. "How did you guys end up here? And who is that blonde that keeps staring at me?"

Maya and Sanaya shared a look. "That would be Elizabeth, and the longer you stay the more you will get to know her." Sanaya mumbled, not feeling like going into details about Elizabeth's antics.

"I was brought here because my mother was the leader of a strong Voodoo coven," Maya replied sadly. "But all of us possess gifts that the Vatican values, which is the main reason all of us are here."

"So I was told," Trent added. He glanced over at Sanaya. "Aren't you like the slayers of all slayers or somethin'?"

When she didn't immediately answer, he continued. "On the way here, one of the guardians told me all about you. Said you are like the first in over a thousand years. I thought with a title like that over ya head, you would be the most popular one up in here."

"Well, popularity is not something I care for and if that is what you are seeking, then you need to sit with the crazy blonde and her crew." Sanaya grumbled, not looking at him.

He glanced over at Elizabeth who met his gaze with a smile. He ignored it. "Nah, I'm cool. I'm more of a low key person myself. " When he was finished, he pushed his plate to the side of the table. Students were already leaving, and Sanaya knew it was a matter of minutes before her escorts came.

"So, where can I find yall?" He said finally, offering them a warm, perfect smile. "I mean, it ain't fun being new and not knowing anything."

"Maya and I typically hang in the courtyard between classes." Sanaya offered.

"You got a phone yet?" Maya asked, pulling out her phone.

"Yeah. They gave it to me as soon as I got here." The three of them exchanged numbers before the Guardian, Tia, returned to retrieve Trent.

"Alright young man, time's up." She said checking her watch. "Sanaya, Eve is outside waiting for you."

"Ok." Sanaya grabbed her plate and stepped away from the table.

"I'mma check yall out later," Trent replied offering them a smile. He then mentally nudged Sanaya, demonstrating his own telepathic abilities. She gazed at him, eyes wide with surprise.

See you later, Slayer. His smile caused her to look away, masking a huge grin that threatened to expose itself.

He trotted off behind Tia, disappearing behind the double doors that connected to another section of the building.

I think he likes me 'Naya, Maya teased.

Sanaya shrugged. *He IS fine…But let's get out of here before Archer comes in with reinforcements. You know how he is.*

CHAPTER SEVEN

Daemon relaxed idly on the black leather sectional, directly across from the freshly lit fireplace, legs crossed, dressed in an all-black Armani suit and a pair of slip on calf-skins from the line's recent inventory. He sipped from his wine glass filled with blood, still warm from the recent kill and eyed the master vampire standing next to the bar curiously. Ronan was the vampire's name, and one of Daemon's protégés, and perhaps the most ambitious of them all.

"I found her sire," Ronan announced after a moment of silence.

"I know," Daemon replied coolly before taking another sip of blood.

"I have even mind locked with her," Ronan added carefully. He shifted his position against the bar and waited for Daemon's response.

"Foolish move Ronan," Daemon sighed. "The Guardians will come for you and I am not in the position to create any more masters!" Daemon tossed the wine glass, still filled with blood and watched it shatter against the pristine white walls of the master's apartment.

Ronan recoiled and prepared himself for an immediate extermination by the ancient vampire, but when Daemon remained in his seat, Ronan relaxed only slightly. His instincts still kept him on the edge. Daemon was not one to bestow acts of mercy and in this case, there was still the ever present possibility that this may be his last night of existence.

"We can use this to our advantage," Ronan began carefully. "We can use this to draw her out. We can infiltrate The Academy through her being that she is still young and gullible. We can cause division in their ranks."

"And what will you do should she come to you of her own will? Answer me this Ronan: she is immune to our bites, so she will not turn. She has not, however, reached the age of maturity where there is a window of fertility that renders her vulnerable. The most you can do is kill her, which is not exactly within the agenda of our Dark Lord. So what will you do Ronan?"

"I…uh..."

"Have acted foolishly. I simply instructed you to watch, not mindlock with her and implement your own strategy!" Daemon dematerialized from the sectional and reappeared in front of Ronan in less than a blink and slammed the weaker vampire against the glass counter of the bar, shattering it.

"Give me one reason why I should not exterminate your incompetent ass this moment, and please, entertain me," Daemon growled, pressing his now almost seven inch fangs against the master's jugular.

"I can use her to lure the other young guardians," he rattled off quickly. "Those who are not immune to our bites, we can diminish the Guardian ranks by targeting the fledgling Guardians, thus weakening her resolve. If we do this steadily, by the time she turns twenty- one she will be emotionally and spiritually broken and easy targets for whatever the Dark Lord's plans are."

Daemon relaxed his grip and retracted his fangs. "Your suggestion has merit. However, we already have someone in place to infiltrate and break her spirit as you have mentioned, but targeting the younger inexperienced Guardians will definitely have The Academy divided." Daemon released him and took a step back to allow Ronan to collect himself.

Ronan adjusted the collar of his navy button down and smoothed out his slacks and cleared his throat. His pale citrine eyes met the abysmal darkness that illuminated from Daemon's and smiled wickedly. "I can pick the guardians off one by one," he offered. "And when the time comes for her to choose, she will not have much to choose from."

"I give you full permission to terrorize The Academy," Daemon concluded. "would result in tossing your carcass into the streets at dawn, or worse. The Guardians have proven themselves throughout the centuries to be worthy adversaries, and now is not the time for the empire to lose valuable resources."

"I understand sire."

"Good. And Ronan?" Daemon quizzed as he transformed into vapor.

"Yes?"

"I will be watching you very closely. Try to mate her before it is time and I will personally rip out your entrails and feed them to the wolves. Understood?" With that, Daemon disappeared into the night on a mission to continue the agendas of the Darkness Organization, but his own.

■■■

Sanaya and Maya met with Eve just outside of the hall, and as promised, both were met with a full Guardian escort ushering the two girls into the center of the group. All nationalities and races were represented by the seven Guardians, which made Sanaya wonder what each of their own personal stories were. One of the Guardians in particular being a huge six foot nine giant, with the nickname Congo, who guarded her from her right. Dark as the African sky on its blackest night, with a scar running vertically from his left eye to his cheek; he walked with the quiet cool swagger of a man who'd seen it all and done it all but was fortunate enough to talk about it. She'd seen him in passing a few times, and she knew he worked with the guardians responsible for dealing with the high level entities such as werewolves and vampires. He kept his eyes focused ahead of them, armed with several blades strapped to his utility belt, and dressed in military fatigues with his semi-automatic assault rifle, Sanaya knew without a doubt he would be one of the guardians on the hunt for the master vampire, and cringed at the thought.

They first walked to Maya's dorm where she was told to grab a few of her things before heading to Sanaya's room where she was instructed to do the same. Afterwards, they headed to the main building, next to the main chapel of the church and they were quickly ushered inside to the second floor. Sanaya shot Maya a nervous glance when they were finally left alone with just Eve and Congo in a spacious room, decorated with a small dining table, a flat screen facing a small sectional with two adjoining rooms offering a shared bathroom between the two.

Looks like a hotel room Maya, Sanaya mentally shot to her best friend.

I know right? I guess this is where we will be staying, Maya responded as she dropped her black and yellow duffle bag on the freshly polished hard wood floor.

"So ladies," Congo began, crossing his massive arms against his chest. "This is where you two will be holed up until the situation is resolved."

For some reason, the subtle reminder that a master vampire was tracking her brought on a new sense of dread. Sanaya eased her bag onto the floor and wrapped her arms around herself, leaning against the door frame.

"We're going vampire hunting," Congo declared, offering her a reassuring grin. "This will all be over before you know it."

"I hope so," Sanaya slowly exhaled, still leaning against the door frame.

"Alright, well I'm out. Gotta strap up for tonight," Congo said, smoothing a palm over his bald head.

"Thanks Congo," Eve replied warmly, flashing him her perfect grin.

"Keep smiling at me like that Eve and I-"

"Let's remain appropriate in front of our impressionable slayer and young guardian," Eve scolded playfully, ushering the megalith of a human out of the room.

"I'm just saying Eve. Archer is gonna have to-"

"Archer is gonna have to do what?"

Sanaya's eyes widened when she heard the voice of her mentor approaching from the hall. Her eyes met Maya's instantly. *So there is something going on between Archer and Eve...*

Maya simply nodded, her eyes lit with amusement as they both continued to watch Congo tease Archer.

"Archer is gonna have to do what?" Sanaya's guardian repeated.

Congo barked out a laugh. "All I'm saying is this bro, you are slippin'. I will risk a vein any night-"

"Thanks Congo," Eve interrupted before all of the playful banter disappeared. Eve gently pushed Congo from the doorway, encouraging him to go on his way. Archer remained in near the entryway, his expression hard and Sanaya knew that Archer was far from amused. Fortunately, Congo was intelligent enough to continue with his exodus, lest Archer decides to take it a step further.

"Ok, ladies well as Congo said, this is where you will camp out for the time being," Eve stated as she collapsed on the sectional, crossing her long legs.

"This is one of the many guest rooms The Academy hosts for visiting Guardians when the need arises. The two windows which overlook the campus are barred, which means nothing can get in or out unless the individual is crazy strong and," Archer glanced at Sanaya. "As talented as you are, I am confident that you are not that damn strong yet." He waited for Sanaya to respond and when all she did was roll her eyes, he continued. "The room is armed with a few silver tipped stakes that are hidden underneath the floor boards in the bedrooms. All water that is filtered in here is blessed, coming through silver pipelines. Each room has a mini fridge, and you are welcomed to whatever is in it. Eve and

Tia have first watch, while a small group of us begin tracking." He cleared his throat and ran an anxious hand over his freshly shaved head. "So that is it in a nutshell I guess."

"If the vampire cannot breach the school," Sanaya began, striving to sound as calm as possible. "Why all of the precautions?"

Archer swallowed thickly and looked away. "Eve is better suited to explain that part to you. Just trust me when I say it is for your own safety." Without another word, Archer excused himself from the room leaving Eve alone with the two teenagers.

"Well," Eve said after a beat. "That was interesting…a lot to process."

"So let's cut to the chase," Maya pressed, placing a hand on her hip. "What's up with this vampire? If he can't appear on campus and attempt to snatch 'Naya, then what do we have to worry about?"

"Masters are different than the run of the mill vampire. Not only are they stronger, faster and armed with seemingly unlimited powers and abilities, they are extremely sensual. As a matter of fact since we are on the subject, vampires and sexuality are essentially one and the same. Every action taken from the stalking of their prey to the actual delivery of the bite offers a high level of eroticism for them. A master's power comes from the darkest of sources, and all levels of sexuality stems from that. We are concerned about Sanaya for many reasons. One, they are not supposed to know that you exist and we may have accidentally tipped our hand in their favor and alerted them to your presence. It is one thing to kill a regular vampire, but another to fight a master." Eve paused, mentally examining the girls before continuing. She noticed Sanaya's deer in the headlights expression and knew she'd hit the nail on the head. "Two, the fact that he has mind locked with Sanaya, he has a sort of supernatural GPS on her, so let's say if she did leave the campus tonight for any reason, she would not be safe. He would track her, and kill whoever was in her company. The great thing is he can't turn her but, there are other ways you can be killed or worse, he can attempt to hold you hostage until you mature, and…there is just a whole lot he can do to you to promote his own agenda."

"So basically, this all boils down to sex?" Maya asked.

"Maya!" Sanaya scolded, burying her face in her hands.

Maya shrugged. "Well is it?"

"Yes and no," Eve responded calmly. "Sanaya, he is going to do everything in his power to seduce you out of The Academy. It is another tactic masters use on their prey. Once locked in your mind he is going to become the object of your sexual fantasies to the point of madness and you will do anything to break out of here and find him. He will become your beacon of relief and will remain so until he is exterminated." Eve bit her lip nervously. "That is why I'm here. I know how to lessen the tie energetically, and to make sure that should he decide to call you," Eve met Sanaya's gaze. "You don't run."

The silence that accompanied Maya's gasp reiterated to Sanaya that her nerves were on edge, and she needed to be in motion. Pushing herself from the door frame, she swiftly slipped into the first bedroom, locking the door behind her. A moment was all she needed, at least that is what she told herself. Sinking to the floor, she folded her knees, wrapping her arms around them in a huddled position as she'd done when she first arrived to The Academy. People were going to die. She knew it. Guardians weren't invincible. She was the one destined to hunt masters and all of the stronger levels of darkness, and yet here she was yet again in another position where she felt…helpless. Sucking in a deep breath, she allowed the anxiety to wash over her.

What is wrong with me? She swallowed thickly and rested her head against the door. *Why is this-*

"Naya?" Maya's concerned voice interrupted Sanaya's thoughts followed by a soft rap on the door.

"Naya? Are you ok?"

"Yeah," Sanaya said pushing herself up off of the floor. "I just needed a moment to digest everything."

"Can I come in?"

Sanaya slowly reached for the handle and opened the door. Eve was still seated on the couch, but was heavily engaged on her cell, while Maya slipped in taking a seat on the edge of the queen sized bed in the center of the room.

"You know they won't allow that vampire to get to you, right?"

Sanaya exhaled sharply. "That is not what I am worried about Maya. I'm the one that is supposed to kill him-"

"But you're not ready! We are not ready-"

"People are going to die Maya!"

Maya flinched at Sanaya's panicked outburst. "They are Guardians 'Naya. They have been doing this long before we were even born and have done so throughout the centuries when there wasn't a slayer."

"But this time Maya," Sanaya began as she paced the room. "This time I think things are different."

"How so?"

"I don't know...I just do. Something's telling me that all of this just ain't right."

Suddenly, the door swung open drawing both girls' attention. Eve poked her head in with a warm smile.

"Are you girls alright?"

"Yeah, uh…we're fine," Sanaya said mentally pleading for Maya to remain quiet.

"Just know that are you are safe Sanaya," Eve assured her. "Things will be back to normal before you know it."

"As if any of this is normal," Maya mumbled underneath her breath.

"Well, I will be in the other room if you need me. Tia is on her way and…" Eve held Maya's gaze. "If anything out of the ordinary happens, call me." Eve closed the door behind her, leaving the two girls alone once more.

"Sanaya what are we gonna do?" Maya asked, nervously picking her nails.

"I don't know…I think I should convince Archer to take me on the hunt and allow me to put him down."

"But Sanaya, you're nowhere near ready to go up against a master!" Maya gasped. "Are you insane? If I can recall everything correctly, Archer and Eve had to bring you back."

Sanaya yanked off her scrunchie that held her thick hair in a single ponytail and threw it at the wall in frustration. "Ugh! I know!"

Maya stood up and walked over to her friend, wrapping her arms around her and resting her head on her shoulder, something she instinctively knew to do whenever Sanaya is in panic mode.

"Just chill out 'Naya," she whispered. "We will be kicking vampire ass in no time. But, we can't take unnecessary risks that could get more Guardians killed. You think you're having issues now? Imagine how you'd feel if more of them got hurt because we did something stupid. Just let them do their jobs."

It was rare that Maya offered such sound and rational advice. However, Sanaya welcomed it. She knew her friend was right. Even if Archer did allow her to go out, she was not experienced enough yet to not be a liability of the team and she definitely did not want to be labeled as that. She gently eased her friend away and ran her fingers through her hair.

"Sleeping in here with me tonight in case I get a little coo-coo?"

"You should have known that already," Maya chirped.

"Alright then, well I got first dibs on the shower. I think the SyFy network has some sort of a werewolf marathon coming on in an hour. We might as well get comfortable."

"Girl, you and those freakin' werewolf movies," Maya chuckled shaking her head.

Sanaya paid her friend no mind as she dug into her duffel and pulled out a pair of purple sweats, a tank and her personal toiletries and made her way into the hotel styled bathroom, sending a silent mental prayer of protection around the guardians with the hope that each of them make it back by dawn safely. However, her intuition told her otherwise...

CHAPTER EIGHT

Archer eyed the team of seven guardians that stood before him, sending a silent prayer to the heavens that each one of them makes it back to the campus at dawn in one piece. This was not his first time tracking a master level vampire.However, for two of the members of his team; it was pretty close to it. Shoving his Berretta into its holster, he took one last look at the group of men and women before nodding his head for them to follow him. Times had definitely changed, not only for the Vatican but for the guardian teams around the world. The Slayer was alive and well on the planet during this millennium, not to mention a few years shy of selecting members of her own guardian team and the shit had not even hit the fan yet. It was one thing protecting students and staff from low level vampires, a few demons here and there, and maybe a werewolf gone feral…but now, the threat level had increased tenfold with a master vampire in such close proximity to the adolescent slayer. The stakes had definitely been raised. No pun intended.

They walked quickly, each member hanging closely behind the other only to separate once outside in the parking lot to their own means of transportation. They knew when and where to meet along with the rest of the rules of the game such as no solo hunts or no bringing anything home with them unless it passed the daylight inspection. Two members of the guardian team decided to accompany him to the destination: Halo, the newest addition to the Guardians and fresh out of the Vampire Hunters Academy; a young African American woman in her twenties with a head full of long, platinum dyed locks standing at 5'4", deep mahogany skin with the body of life. Gifted as a tracker, she probably had the best nose on the planet, able to break down scents to their compound levels. Plus, the girl was a master in various styles of martial arts which would indeed render her effective in a fight against the Darkness. The other newbie to the team, an arrogant and former apprentice of a wizard from the dark arts, Stefan, was also new to the battlefield with a master level vampire. The kid was in his mid-twenties and was used by the Vatican more often than not to handle business affairs for the local parishes. Why the Vatican decided to add this kid to the team was a mystery to him, but according to Tia, the kid had some serious skills in hand to hand combat. However, Archer secretly suspected that this kid may end up being the weakest link. Physically, the kid looked like he was born for the warrior class: standing at almost six feet, with a lean swimmer's build from years of participating on the swim team and running track. He kept his dusty brown hair swept back, making sure to keep it no longer than the base of his neck. The kid didn't have any troubles in the lady's department; from what Archer could remember the kid was the talk of the school for quite some time. However, Stefan was a recluse and tended to prefer his own company…and Halo's. Still, whatever skills this kid had at his disposal, he better put them to use tonight.

Master vampires were no easy kills.

With the three of them strapped in, he pulled out of the parking lot, and into the night. The club district would be a war zone and he could only pray that it wasn't one of those popular nights that drew every young person eighteen and older out to play.

The Guardians arrived one by one in front of the crowded two story structure, facing the narrow street. The fast pace beat of techno sounds blaring from the speakers to deafening volumes while adrenaline, perfume, and sex tainted the air, filling the team's nostrils and bludgeoning their palates. Despite all of the normal night life sounds and the electricity that filled the night, the hairs on the back of Archer's neck stood at attention. Halo anxiously checked her revolver multiple times before replacing it on her hip. Congo tensely folded his arms as he rested against a nearby streetlamp and hocked spit onto the sidewalk. Halo scowled at him with disgust but kept her opinion to herself. Archer pretended to feign interest in the club, nodding appreciatively at a few young scantily clad women as they walked by before turning to face his team.

"Earlier today Tia and Eve canvassed the area. The vibe I'm sensing is real thick and seems to be increasing by the minute. Blend in. Keep your eyes open. Watch for any fledglings in the area because as we know, where the masters go the slaves follow. Send a mental SOS should you come across the master, but do not attempt to engage with the bastard solo. We have a couple of newbies rolling with us on their first real hunt so let's show 'em how it's done."

Congo said nothing as he stalked off behind Olivia, Shawn, and Paul towards the entrance of the club. Halo and Stefan remained with Archer as he motioned them to follow him in the shadows where they would lie and wait.

■■■

Sanaya dozed off minutes into the American Werewolf, comforted by the fact that her best friend was in the room with her. The sound of the television blaring was the perfect recipe for a lullaby as she nestled deeper underneath the beige comforter. She vaguely heard Maya's fingers tapping against her phone, obviously engaged in a serious text convo with Sanaya assumed to be the new kid Trent. With her body completely relaxed and her mind drifting away into the welcoming nothingness, it was not long before the voices from the television and Maya's extraordinary texting abilities were no longer her lullabies. She'd completely melted away into the mattress, her mind expanding, stretching well beyond the horizon of the living, creating its own nightly rhythm of worlds ready for her to explore.

From the safety of her own body, she watched herself stroll through the city of Los Angeles, her hometown, recounting the days when her mother was alive and in a rare moment of contentment. Her mother smiled at her as they stopped in their favorite ice cream joint-Cold Stones-and Sanaya's face lit up as she ordered her usual white chocolate ice cream dripping with caramel syrup, peanuts and whipped cream. A quiet longing filled her chest as the memory stabbed into her consciousness, but she refused to give into mourning. Instead, she pretended that all of this was real and she was not the Slayer, but a regular girl having some much needed mother and daughter time as they took a seat in a corner of the eatery overlooking the street. Taking a huge spoonful of the specialty ice cream, she moaned with delight. Her mother watched her, still smiling, having yet to taste her own and that is when Sanaya realized something wasn't right.

Her mother's once beautiful brown skin melted away into a creamy white, almost porcelain complexion. Her radiantly brown eyes shifted into a pale green, and her immaculately styled coils transitioned into blonde tresses that were slicked back into a long ponytail. A handsome face adorned with highly chiseled cheek bones greeted with a sly grin. Her instincts began firing off, but something else held her in place. He made sure to sustain an image where his perfect pectorals were on display through an opened silk shirt, exposing smooth unmarred flesh that simply begged for her touch. Her breathing became hitched at the full vision of this vampire, a master of illusion and she wondered how she would free herself from this dream turned instant nightmare.

"Good evening Slayer," he said, widening his grin. His heavily accented voice sent a shiver down her spine.

"What do you want?" She demanded, summoning the discipline to resist the call that this vampire's silent message triggered within her body.

"The question is," he began slowly. "What do you want?"

She looked away, gazing out of the window of the familiar street that once brought happiness to her bleak world when everything she knew was normal.

"Cat got your tongue?" He teased, gracefully sliding his hand to where her abandoned ice cream waited. He snatched it effortlessly, taking her spoon and scooping up a mouthful of her favorite ice cream and placing it into his mouth.

She glared at him, bile building up in the back of her throat as she watched the vampire imitate her pleasure that confectionary desert had given her as he moaned, licking the spoon dry.

"I can see why you would appreciate this so," he said sticking the spoon back into the cup. "This particular brand of ice cream is indeed heaven for the taste buds...sinfully sweet...but, nothing compares to the sweet taste that makes you, you..."

Sanaya's heart raced as her adrenaline spiked, giving her the fuel she needed to jump up and break the leg from the chair to brandish a stake. The master was on his feet instantly, and before she could act with the stake in his chest, he gripped her wrists and transported them through any dimension of her dream. She was naked, and pinned beneath his massive body in what appeared to be his lair. Black marble met crimson velvet while she struggled against his grasp.

"You smell divine young one," He groaned, placing a kiss on the side of her throat. "Submit to me..."

"No!"

A low growl rumbled in the center of his chest. "Submit to me. I cannot take you like this!"

"No!" Tears of frustration filled her eyes as she mentally prayed to wake up.

He forced her arms above her head, his neon green eyes illuminating in the darkness of his lair. "If you do not come to me of your own will, then those Guardians who dare themselves strong enough to hunt me will meet their end, as will every student at your Academy. You *will* bend to me Slayer or you will watch everyone you love *die!*"

He disappeared the instant her eyes snapped open. She sat up with a jolt, screaming in terror. She heard Maya's yell for help and she could feel her calming hands smoothing her messy hair back from her face. She felt like she was still trapped in the dream, despite Eve's strong hands gripping her by the shoulders and shook her; however she struggled and fought against her hold. Tia's voice could be heard calling her name, but nothing could break her from the cold terror that threaten to siphon all of her sanity. The fact remained that Archer and his team of Guardians were in trouble if she didn't do something. The entire Academy was in trouble if she didn't act.

"He is coming," she finally whispered.

"Who is coming?" Tia demanded.

"Archer is in danger. Call the Guardians back!" Sanaya screamed, panic strengthening her enough to break free of Eve's hold.

"Sanaya!" Maya hollered, chasing after her.

Still in a grip of terror, Sanaya dodged her best friend and ran out of the room in search of a weapon. Eve reached her before she could yank the floorboards of the living room back and slapped her with such a force that her neck snapped back.

"Sanaya," Eve demanded. "Sanaya!"

Although no longer caught in the panicked daze, instant fatigue blanketed her as she went limp, collapsing into Eve's embrace.

"He said if I do not come to him of my own free will he will kill the guardians that hunt him as well as the students from the Academy," Sanaya sobbed. "I can't let him do that."

Eve and Tia shared a knowing glance, before Tia finally said, "I'm calling Archer. They've been set up."

Congo remained seated at the bar, his dark skin prickling from the vibrations of something that just wasn't right. He could sense the nervousness in the other guardians as they patrolled the scene, pretending to be just regular clubbers, when he tasted the evil that tainted the air on his palate. Demons. And perhaps a legion of them were manifesting into semisolid form. Rogue wolves corrupted by the darkness and of course the freshly transitioned vampires surrounded this place. The Master Vampire clearly was a shrewd son of a bitch, and Congo flexed both of his massively thick arms and popped his joints, anxious to claim the kill of one the top motherfuckers in the supernatural food chain. Paul approached him with Olivia and Shawn behind him when all of their cell phones went off at once with a message from Tia.

Yo, fall back. It's a trap.

"No shit," Congo grumbled to himself. "Let's bounce. This is some bullshit."

Just then gun shots were heard outside, which meant that Archer and the two newbies may be in some trouble. However, as more shots rang out, the music in the club came to an immediate halt as its human patrons went into panic mode. Several rogue wolves shifted in the center of a large crowd of onlookers and immediately attacked several unsuspecting victims. Paul and Shawn were on them in an instant, hitting the beasts with round after round of silver which separated them from their victims and incinerating them on contact. Piles of sulfuric ash clouded the scene as dozens of innocents ran for their lives.

Congo spotted a freshly turned vampire, perhaps no older than twenty at the time of his death snatch a pretty brown eyed girl from the crowd and sink his four inch incisors into her throat. She screamed as Congo head straight for them with his silver dagger in hand, decapitating the vampire in the process. The young woman fell to the ground, her body undergoing multiple seizures and slipping into shock. Congo hated what he had to do next. He placed the silver dagger into the center of her chest, putting an end to the turn but also her life. He said a quick prayer over her body and secretly hoped that her spirit had been made right enough to ascend. However, he did not have time to contemplate the ramifications of what a sinful life could bring because he found himself surrounded by dozens of demon entities ranging in size and level of grotesqueness. From his holster he pulled out two mini Uzi's and unleashed a fury of silver, their high pitched screeching causing his ears to bleed.

More screams entered his consciousness as he ushered the last remaining innocents out into the street. The dark presence, an entity stronger than those that currently terrorized the club, slammed into his psyche followed by the telepathic SOS from Olivia. Just beyond the DJ booth, she struggled with Shawn to lift an injured Paul. Apparently, Paul tried to rescue a couple of underage patrons from a group of vampires. Not only was he overwhelmed, but he ran out of ammo. Olivia was too busy working on the alpha wolf while Shawn had been on the other side of the club beating back his own vamp problem. Olivia fought back unshed tears; her heart shaped face flushed beet red with anger.

"He's turning man!" She screamed in panic. "Oh God not Paul!"

"If we can get him to the Vatican in time he just might have a chance," Congo replied as calmly as possible, unsure if he believed his own words.

They hurried outside, shooting at anything without a pulse in range when they found Archer standing just a few yards away from an entity that had bulked up in size preparing to fight. In front of him lay the now deceased young Guardian Stefan, with Halo sobbing over his body. The entity quickly turned to greet the new additions to the party, flashing one of the longest sets of incisors Congo had ever seen. This was indeed the Master. Something had drawn him out to play.

Archer, Congo, Olivia, and Halo surrounded the entity with Shawn discreetly guiding Paul to the car.

"You hide the girl," The vampire stated confidently. His once neon green eyes a deep crimson. "Give her to me or your entire team dies."

"Fuck you!" Archer spat as he shot a silver tipped arrow directly at the entity's chest.

The other Guardians followed suit and the master dodged all of their attempts effortlessly. He shifted into mist, reappearing in solid form in front of Halo. Archer, using his skills in marital arts flung silver coated death stars that slammed the master in various sections of his chest. However, that was not enough to stop the entity. He snatched Halo by the neck and disappeared. The team of Guardians lost it, shooting everything they had into the vapor.

Halo was gone. Stefan was gone. And if they didn't Paul back to the Vatican in time, he would be too. Archer cursed and kicked over trash bin, while Olivia fell to her knees and wailed. They had indeed been set up, and Archer as head Guardian could not rest with the fact that he had been overconfident in his strategy. Every Master differed in strength and ability depending on the age and the strength of the vampire that made them. This particular Master was perhaps much stronger than the ones he encountered previously. He should have taken more Guardians and left the two newbies at The Academy.

None of the remaining Guardians spoke as each headed towards their separate vehicles: with Shawn and Olivia riding with Paul. The procedure would be for the team to transport a wounded Guardian to a local cathedral where a specially trained priest would use every blessed ritual including the usage of holistic medicines to rid the Guardian of the toxins that threatened his or her humanity. Archer knew there would be at least 50/50 chance that Paul would survive. He needed to make it through the first three days without the blood hunger before the Vatican could exhale in relief.

But that, unfortunately, was the least of their problems. The Master was still alive and Halo would more than likely join his harem of lair mates, which meant that they would have to put her down too. Archer shook his head. And Sanaya…that may be the reason why Tia called.

CHAPTER NINE

Sanaya awakened to the sounds of Archer's fervent whispers in the front room. Maya was still unconscious, gripping her pillow and Tia must have stepped out. She sat up, shoving the blankets out of her way, the memories from last night's experience flooding into her awareness. Panic threatened to reveal itself as she expanded her senses into the front room, desperate to discover what happened. What the vampire threatened was real and if Archer was here in the other room, speaking to Eve in hushed tones, she had more than enough reason to believe that last night did not go exactly as planned.

"Halo..." she heard him say, his voice cracking. "The fucker just snatched her and vanished. And, it was entirely my fault. She was in my charge. I should have-"

"Don't think like that Archer," Eve soothed. "Don't. She made her choice when she overheard you discussing the opportunity. We all make a choice each time we go out into the field. It is our job-"

"And then Paul man...Paul and I finished training together. He had just as much experience as me when they got him. I should have taken more Guardians! Our team was too small...now, the man is fighting for his life and from the looks of it, and he won't survive the next three days. We were too late..."

Sanaya had never heard her Guardian ward sound so defeated. He was always confident, strutting around like the entire universe was in the palm of his hands. She covered her mouth with her hand to prevent the sob that threatened to reveal her presence. But the fact remained that two and perhaps three Guardians were dead, all because of her. No wonder her peers hated her. They knew that seven of them will be the unfortunate chosen to join in her quest against the Darkness which would mean she would be sentencing them to death. She had to do something. The next time the vampire met her in her dreams she would be ready for him. She would put an end to this, and then, she was leaving the Academy.

She moved away from the door and to the bathroom where she washed her face and brushed her teeth. Class would begin in an hour, and she was certain that she and Maya would be escorted by a full Guardian team on top of having to deal with Archer being all over their case for every little thing. She took out her wide tooth comb and made an angled part in the front section of her hair, and smoothing it down with the gel she had to have specially ordered from the states before piling the rest of her hair back in a bun. She could sense Maya awakening, which prompted her to hurry. She threw on a pair of black denim and a navy blue top, still unable to shake the anxiety that crept into her psyche.

When she finally emerged from the bathroom, dressed and anxious to go, Maya was sitting up, stretching out her arms, yawning deeply. Neither said a word to each other as Maya took her place in the bathroom, to which Sanaya was grateful. There was just too much to think about, and the images of last night's nightmare permeated her senses. She could still smell the vampire's foul breath as he pressed his cold hard body against hers demanding entry. She shuddered. The vampire's will revealed itself to be strong, powerful even. She swallowed thickly, mentally vowing to strengthen her own will. Besides, losing her virginity to a master vampire, a blood sucking demon; a curse upon mankind was *not* something she planned on doing. Ever. And she definitely was not about to be pressured into something she wasn't ready for, no matter how pretty the package.

Fuck that.

Fifteen minutes later, Eve gently opened the door, her expression sullen as she took one look at Sanaya.

"Are you girls almost ready?" She asked, taking note that Maya was still in the bathroom.

"Maya should be ready soon," Sanaya replied evenly. "Is everything alright?"

Eve shook her head. "Please tell her to hurry. We have to escort you to breakfast early so we can make it in time for the meeting. Things…" Eve's gaze quickly shot to the floor. "Things did not go well last night."

Sanaya inhaled deeply, fighting back tears. "This is all my fault."

Eve hurried away from the door and grabbed her by her shoulders, forcing Sanaya to gaze into her hypnotically blue stare.

"No it is not. The Guardians…" Eve sighed. "They were not prepared. This master is different and evidently aligned with multiple entities from the dark world."

"But-" Sanaya pleaded.

"No buts Sanaya." Eve's voice grew firm. "We expected more encounters from The Darkness the moment you arrived to The Academy. It comes with the territory of guarding a Slayer. And, it is only going to become worse as you get older because your scent, your energy will grow and they will have the ability to root you out. Everything about you is supposed to draw them in, vampires especially, so we knew this would happen. We knew the risks from the beginning. Now our job is to put that son of a bitch out of his misery while you train hard and learn as much as you can because…" Eve lowered her voice to a near whisper. "The world needs you now more than ever."

They stood in companionable silence until the door to the bathroom twisted an unlocked, and a freshly showered Maya came strolling out. Her silky, naturally wavy hair was hanging loosely passed her shoulders, being pulled back with a purple head band. She wore a pair of loosely fitted camos and a black top with black Timberlands, looking like she was ready for war.

"Are you ready Maya?" Sanaya asked her friend as she shoved her things into her duffle bag.

"Yep, ready as ever." Maya turned to face Eve and Sanaya, examining their somber expressions.

"Are you guys alright? What happened? Did they get the vampire?"

Eve sighed. "C'mon you two. I think it is best if Sanaya tells you."

Maya glanced at Sanaya with a raised brow. tThere was nothing more for Sanaya to do other than shrug. Sanaya knew that it frustrated her friend to no end to not be included in on the details of every situation involving Guardian business. Sanaya followed behind Eve without waiting for Maya to catch up. Maya should have known by now that Sanaya would always fill her in.

Another wave of dread flooded Sanaya's senses as they headed down the hall to meet with three additional Guardians, and all Sanaya could think about was how much worse things could get as soon as night fell.

■■

Petronius rested against the elaborately stitched gold fabric of his comforter as he prepared to rest while the merciless rays of the sun blazed across the horizon. He'd spent the night feeding off the blood of several young women from one of the many organized rings of human trafficking he orchestrated inside his multimillion dollar mansion overlooking the Hudson River. His human helpers, of course, spared no expense in delivering the human women to his doorstep before escorting them through the heavily fortified halls of his estate. Escape was impossible. Sound proofing-a requirement. Their screams of terror only heightened his thirst; their fear spiked adrenaline making their blood much more potent. And by the time he had finished gorging himself silly on the dozens of spiritually broken and abused women, the sun had begun to rise over the horizon. His body responded with overwhelming fatigue despite the surrounding darkness that his lair provided.

Settling into his four poster king sized bed, he relaxed, enjoying the flow of the blood of his victims filtering through his veins, strengthening him. He was semiconscious when he received a phone call from the landline that rested next to him on the nightstand. He shot up, irritated with the disruption of his rest, his normally dark eyes now glowing crimson as he snatched the phone from the receiver.

"This better be worth disturbing me from my slumber," Petronius hissed.

"And so the dragon is still awake," Alex wheezed with a chuckle.

"Tell me brother, does insomnia plague you?"

"No, it is not insomnia that ails me brother," Alex quipped. "It is concern. Even though my eyes may fail me, my ears have not and it is not like you to be unaware of such atrocities taking place against your Slayer…"

Petronius leaned forward, his fangs lengthening. "What are you rambling about?"

"It has been reported that a member of the Guardian team that protects the slayer has been compromised."

"You LIE!"

"You flatter me brother," Alex rasped. "But no."

"We have not been sanctioned to make any more vampires! This has the potential to be problematic and catastrophic to our plans. Who is responsible?"

"A young master by the name of Ronan I believe."

"Ronan? Who is his sire?"

"That has yet to be discovered."

"This changes things. Send out your best spies to discover more about this Ronan character as well as his maker. Leave no stone unturned."

"And what will you do?"

Petronius paused, reflecting on the new insight proposed to him. "I will activate the mole my brother. I think it is time for The Guardians to begin recruiting again."

CHAPTER TEN

By the time the last class for the day was over, Sanaya could not be any happier to see her Guardian escort. Not only was she physically drained from the hard core offensive training and sparring with one of the senior members of the Guardian team, but struggling to fight off the anxiety of what is to come as soon as night fell, and of course the usual verbal judo with Elizabeth during lunch and dinner hours, she wasn't sure how long it would take before she would crack from a nervous breakdown. To make matters worse, Trent was paired with her in almost all of her classes and as much as she liked him, she had bigger problems. Plus, with Trent in the picture, giving her the googly eyes, the green eyed monster was beginning to rear its ugly head in Maya and the last thing she needed was her best friend upset with her over a boy.

Sanaya swung her backpack over her shoulders and hurried out of the auditorium where fifty or so of her peers mingled with one another, a few offering friendly glances in her direction. Ignoring them, slipped out of the side exit where Eve waited for her by the benches. Well, Eve and Trent. Eve smiled warmly as Sanaya approached.

"Hello Slayer," Eve chirped.

"Hey Sanaya," Trent added, eyeing her appreciatively.

"Hey guys," Sanaya replied cautiously. "Where's Maya?"

Eve met Sanaya's questioning gaze uneasily.

"She has already been escorted to her room," Eve finally replied evenly.

She's mad at me isn't she? Sanaya mentally shot to Eve who responded with a nod.

But, I didn't do or say anything to her! Sanaya dropped her backpack onto the pavement. *Like, what the heck is her deal?*

Slayer, you have a lot to learn in a short period of time. Maya will come around. She was willing to accept the fact that she would always have to be in your shadow, but I think this young man's interest in you may have put things in perspective for her. She will come around.

Eve gently placed her hand on Sanaya's shoulder. "Let's get you to your room."

Sanaya simply nodded as three more Guardians approached. When Tia approached, her beautiful onyx mane now shaved into a Mohawk style, her expression was unreadable.

"So, we're watching over another kid?" She asked, eyeing Trent suspiciously.

Eve sighed. "He is with me."

Tia and the other Guardians said nothing as they took formation around Sanaya, with Trent walking shoulder to shoulder with her.

"Soooo," Sanaya began, unsure of what to say.

"So, what's going on? Why the protective measures?" Trent asked curiously.

Sanaya shrugged. "It just comes with the territory."

"So what's it like?"

Sanaya tried to keep her eyes focused on the Guardian in front of her. "What's what like?"

Now it was his turn to shrug. "You know…the Slayer thing."

Sanaya inhaled sharply. "It isn't exactly all that, nothing but a bunch of pressure to be all that everyone says that I am, losing my parents,even though they weren't exactly parent material, and being forced to leave behind everything that I knew just to come to a place where everyone except the Guardian staff and the Pope hates my guts. So yeah, real great stuff."

"I think they just don't understand...when I was growing up in the streets, I knew I was different. I saw shit-" Tia's heat seeking glare cut Trent off before he cleared his throat and apologized. "Excuse me, saw stuff that no one else saw. People didn't like me because I would tell them what was coming and when it did happen, they were angry with me as if I was the reason why I brought it to their door in the first place. It happened with each of the foster homes I was in, which is how I ended up having to fend for myself for a little while."

"I'm so sorry Trent."

"Don't be. It is what it is, but that may be why the other students feel the way they do towards you. There would not be any need for Guardians or potential Guardians if Slayers did not exist."

Righteous indignation almost choked her. "There would be no need for slayers if there was no such thing as vampires, or demons, or werewolves or any of that supernatural shi-crap that I am supposed to fight!"

Suddenly, a pair of warm hands were rubbing her back. Sanaya didn't need to turn around to know that it was Eve.

"Well, I know you don't know me but like if you ever need a friend to talk to…"

"Thanks Trent."

They walked for an additional ten minutes before Sanaya detected the presence of someone new. And male. Very male. And angry. The moment she opened her third eye, the connection was imminent and she saw his face. Smooth ebony skin, with dark eyes that glowered at the Guardians who were trying to reason with him. Exposed, muscled and heavily tattooed arms. His expression softened when he sensed her presence, and began to look around frantically.

"Sanaya, leave it alone. He is not someone you should worry about." Tia muttered, loud enough for her to hear.

"She's getting too strong too quickly," came the concerned voice of another Guardian.

"I couldn't help the connection," Sanaya whimpered quietly.

"I know," Eve reassured her.

"Sanaya, are you good?" Trent asked, holding her gaze.

"Yeah…I'm ok."

Eve gave her shoulder a reassuring squeeze while Trent reached for her hand.

No, she was not alright…whoever that young man is being held captive by the Guardians felt the same way she did in that very moment: trapped.

∎∎∎

Archer slammed his fist into the stucco wall of his office where he was supposed to be finishing off the reports of the events that took place last night. But frustration held him in its grip as he thought about the two young Guardians and the senior Guardian that were never again going to return home to whatever family waited for them. Paul did not make it. By the time they made it to the Cathedral, the virus had already settled in his system and began the transition; when the priest went to lay the symbol of the Holy cross against his forehead, Paul went into multiple seizures, his eyes changing from the normal hazel green to an unnatural crimson red before finally slipping into a coma. Being that all of the Guardians present considered Paul family, one of the Church's assassins had to behead him, which left Olivia and Shawn inconsolable.

Congo stormed off, the muscles in his jaw twitching; while all Archer could do was bury his face in his hands.

Now he had to figure out the next step towards putting a stake in the center of the master vampire's chest to ensure Sanaya's future as the Slayer, but not at the expense of the lives of the Guardians. He exhaled sharply, running a hand over his shaven scalp. The Church's head leaders, including the Pope wanted an audience later on in the evening, not to mention there were several new recruits to the school that required his attention, especially the most recent addition, a hard headed, short tempered kid from the streets of Atlanta. Yeah, that was about to be a walk in the park...

Paul's funeral was scheduled for the day after tomorrow and thankfully the only family he left behind was the team of Guardians. Stefan's funeral had yet to be planned due to his family residing on the other side of the globe in the Hamptons and Halo's. Well, there wasn't a body to bury...yet.

"For Christ sake can we just get a break!" Plopping onto his office seat, he leaned back and closed his eyes. Relocating Sanaya to another Guardian stronghold may be their best bet, or their worse mistake ever. Obviously, The Darkness was watching and now, they had not only her scent but her physical identity. A small team of Guardians would never be able to fight off what might be coming in Sanaya's direction, not only a master vampire. That ancient sect of Hell's worse of the worse will send everything they've got to ensure the survivability of evil. As he began to drift off into the higher realms of frustration, he sensed Sanaya's probe into the undisclosed New Recruit Room a few doors down.

And there lies another problem...

Sanaya may well become a fully matured Slayer before her twenty first birthday for reasons Heaven has yet to disclose. Archer never professed to be a man of great prayers, as he felt Sanaya's telepathy cross the barriers of seasoned Guardians, now was a better time more than ever to find that quiet   place in his head and commune with On High. Just then, his cell vibrated across the table. He knew who was on the other line without having to glance at the screen. Swiping his thumb across the screen he sighed as he answered.

"Yes?"

The evening couldn't get any worse.

▪▪

Sanaya almost jumped for joy when Eve insisted on escorting Trent to his room first. Of course he protested, arguing that it was important for a future Guardian to learn the protocol for protecting a Slayer, and of course he was shot down by not only Eve but Tia as well. Naturally, upon delivering him to his room, he immediately sent Sanaya a multitude of text messages, all of which she ignored. It wasn't until she finally put some distance between herself and Trent that she realized that his attraction was based on *what* she is, and not *who* she is which made her more miserable. Maya could have him for all she cared; and the fact that her best friend forever caught a 'tude with her over some boy drama had become too much.

The escort back to the overly secured, Hilton-like room felt like an eternity, and when she finally dumped her things on the hardwood floors, Eve took a seat in the dining room while Tia plopped on the couch. A new duo was supposed to switch shifts with them tonight, and Sanaya meant to take advantage of the situation by isolating herself in her room. Locking the door behind her, she moved to take a seat on the edge of the bed when she felt the connection to the angry young man that was brought in by the Guardians.

I don't know what I am going to do, came the thoughts of the freshly wounded soul of a potential guardian. *Been seeing shit all my life...where were these so called "Guardians" when my folks needed them? Where were they as my ass was being hauled off into a rundown foster home with a crack head for a foster mom and a pimp for a foster father?*

Sanaya's eyes watered from her own pain of having to endure the constant dysfunction that took place between her parents. Her mother was verbally abusive at times when she'd been drinking. And her father, when he decided to come home, acted as if he wanted nothing to do with her half of the time anyways.

First chance I get I'm out of here...

Good luck with that considering you are all the way in Rome, she accidentally shot back, only realizing what she had done when the thought left her brain.

"Oh shit!" She whispered.

How are you in my head? The young man demanded, his fear and anxiety coating his exchange.

Sanaya froze like a frightened rabbit just before it makes a mad dash to safety before it is pursued by a hungry predator.

Sorry about that, she finally answered. *You were broadcasting so loudly I could not help but respond. The Guardians will teach you how to protect your mind.*

Who are you?

She could feel him searching about in his room as if she were right outside of his door, when in actuality, she was on one side of the campus while he was on another.

*My name is Sanaya...*She carefully informed him.

Are you a Guardian?

No, no. I'm a student...

The name is King.

Sanaya realized that once King became relaxed with the idea of communicating via telepathy, the tension in her own body eased.

*Look, I gotta go…because neither one of us is strong enough to put down our own barrier for this type of thing, it will not be long before one of the Guardians taps in…*she shot to him urgently.

Wait! Don't go just yet…where can I find you?

In the courtyard, Sanaya found herself saying. *You can always find me in the courtyard underneath the Willow tree…*

Just then Eve pounded on the door, forcing Sanaya to break the connection and to hurry over to the door to see what all the fuss was about. Inhaling deeply she could only hope that Eve or Tia did not pick up on the mental convo she had with the newbie, King. Opening the door, the expression on Eve's face told her everything she needed to know.

■■

King wrestled against the sheets as he struggled to settle his mind, his senses overwhelmed by his new environment and the reality of his new life. That soothing voice in his head he conversed with and seemed to be listening to his thoughts had finally given him the reprieve that he now resented. Now the Guardians wanted to embrace him into the fold. Now The Academy thought of him as a potential asset to the Light. But where were they when his parents were ripped apart by a pack of demon possessed werewolves? Where were the angels when he prayed for a better opportunity after he was placed in a fucked up foster home with abandoned and abused kids. He was supposed to go to The Academy years ago as his parents planned. He was supposed to be one of the strongest Guardians by this stage of the game. He was already born with incredible gifts, gifts that even surpassed that of his parents.

But he was left behind to rot in the system until his last stint in the streets landed him in so much trouble he was facing adult charges.

Illegal possession of a firearm. Resisting arrest. Possession of drug paraphernalia. 25 years was what he was facing until the cocky bastard, Archer appeared and all of his charges were mysteriously dropped. But instead of sitting in confinement in some Georgia prison, he was locked in a room at the Vatican. What difference did that make?

Sure he got a little snappy with the Guardians. And so what if he has a quick mouth, his fists were faster. That was what helped him survive in the streets. He already fought off several vampires and a couple of demons on his own *without* backup from the Vatican. Vampires were already taking control of the streets, capitalizing not only on blood but money too. As a matter of fact, he worked for one before and he was sure as shit that the fucker knew what time it was with him. But he was about that paper; those dollar bills; the root of all evil according to the Bible because what job was going to hire and look out for a seventeen year old kid with no home, no family? These snobby ass Guardians thought that they could just come in, rescue him from his "fate" and expect nothing but gratitude when he had been surviving on his own since he was nine? Just like the Vatican and the Pope himself, all of these bastards truly had him fucked up.

He sat up and pushed his shoulder length dreadlocks away from his face. His girlfriend, LaQuanda back home would wonder what the hell happened to him. She wasn't exactly wife material, but she did look out for him: convinced her mother to stay with them for a while until he "got a job"; held his dope for him when asked, and wasn't a bad lay either. He couldn't even call her. The Guardians made sure of that. The bootleg IPhone he was given could only make local calls and the Wi-Fi was limited.

He thought back to the voice in his head: Sanaya is what she called herself. Telepathy wasn't new to him. As a matter of fact he'd been all up in people's heads since he could talk. He just wasn't used to someone else with the ability, and her gift in telepathy was strong, much stronger than his own. He couldn't get a mindlock with anyone here, but somehow she could. He definitely looked forward to meeting with her at the courtyard tomorrow.

Reaching for the outdated phone, he sent a quick text to his assigned mentor, Congo when his stomach growled. He refused to eat earlier and now he was paying for it. Congo quickly responded informing him that he would see what he could do and to sit tight. Flinging the phone across the room, he punched his mattress in frustration. He didn't even have a damn television in his room to idly pass the time, so how the hell could he just sit tight?

There was a sudden shift in the atmosphere that snapped him out of him mental fit. He tuned his hearing to the sounds of boots hitting the marble flooring of the halls. And then an alarm sounded, followed by an unfamiliar Guardian forcing his door open.

"C'mon kid we're moving you," said the platinum blonde bombshell of a Guardian.

"Why? What happened?" He found himself asking as he retrieved his belongings with her assistance.

"Several students have gone missing and we need to move you. Now."

King followed the Guardian out of the tiny dorm room that reminded him of a prison cell, running behind her down several flights of stairs where she accompanied him to another section of the school to where other students were being ushered into a two story building. He scanned the parameter mentally searching for Sanaya's energy signature, when he sensed her approaching surrounded by her own personal guard.

His chest tightened as his mouth went dry and other parts of his body hardened at the sight. And it didn't take a genius to know that she was more than just the average student to have her own personal guard.

~ 82 ~

When her eyes looked up from the ground she seemed to be preoccupied with meeting with his, instant knowing slammed into her, and for a long moment, neither of them spoke, and somehow, he knew that his stay at the Academy was not going to be so bad after all. Her mentor caught on to their shared glance and stepped in front of her and offered him a nasty scowl. She didn't like him and he could dig it. Not many people did. But the shy, reassuring smile Sanaya offered in his direction made it worth it.

CHAPTER ELEVEN

Sanaya awoke to the terrifying reality that three students, second year students to be exact were missing. The Academy was supposed to be a formidable fortress against The Darkness and yet, three sophomores were missing, and no one could figure out how. The only common denominator that three students shared were that they were all linked to Elizabeth Van Helsing's crew; and the reason why the Queen of Spite was spending the morning under heavy interrogation by the leaders of the school. Not to mention there was still the master vampire that was after her, however last night she was given a reprieve from his dreamscape visit and she shuddered to try to figure out why.

Stretching, with a million things on her mind and the burden of the day ahead of her, she checked her phone and still no word from Maya and at least a dozen texts from Trent. She politely replied to Trent's pleas for a response to his worried inquiries before jumping in the shower. Archer was supposed to escort her to breakfast to give Eve a much needed break, and with only forty five minutes to spare Sanaya made sure to move with haste, putting her supernatural abilities to use. Busying herself with her morning ministrations was also a much needed distraction from the seemingly rebellious new potential Guardian, King.

Scrubbing herself with the coconut body scrub Archer ordered for her as a perk, she forced herself not to think about the muscled, lithe frame of the newest Guardian in training; or the intensity of his deep brown eyes when their eyes met, or the commanding presence of his almost six foot frame that loomed over the neighboring students, or those full lips that he licked out of habit that made her forget that she was even breathing. His wife beater exposed an entire sleeve of tattooed pain, and his perfectly smooth, unmarred, and chiseled face with the bone structure that only a skilled artist could replicate was enough to make her weak in the knees. He stared at her as if she were the only one on the planet that mattered...and to her, that mattered. Through their connection he was seeking someone he could relate to; and it was through their connection she realized she too sought the same.

Rinsing off, she was out of the shower when she realized Archer would be knocking on her door in fifteen minutes. She threw on a pair of skinny jeans, a white V-neck and her beige leather jacket and quickly styled her hair into a perfect bun. She was just placing her notebook in her bag when she sensed the familiar presence of her Guardian mentor and rushed to answer the door before he knocked.

"I'm ready," she breathed with her bag in hand and closed the door behind her.

"Good. Glad to know I didn't have to drag you out of the bathroom," he replied evenly. "Did you sleep well?"

Archer studied her quickly, obviously searching for signs of fatigue. Sanaya smiled warmly. "I slept fine surprisingly, considering everything that is going on around here."

"I wouldn't spend too much time worrying about that," he added slowly as they joined the six awaiting Guardians. "The Guardians are working day and night to get to the bottom of things and…"

Archer stopped walking just as they reached the steps leading to an archway facing the acres of greenery that greeted them ahead. "If you hear anything coming from the mouths of the other students that may help in finding those missing students," his hazel eyes held her gaze. "You will let us know, right?"

She nodded, her eyes confirming that her action was a statement of truth. However, there was a part of her that desired to hunt. A surge of an awakening power dawned on her, and she managed to keep it at bay so as not to alert her Guardian mentor. They needed her help whether they wanted to admit it or not; and what they were failing to admit is the fact that hunting is in her blood. She would track those students, even if she had to do it alone, because she reasoned as she fell into formation with the Guardians, this was her fight. Not theirs. And it was time she came out of hiding.

■■

With Elizabeth gone, breakfast was a breeze. Of course, Maya was still not talking to her. She had taken a seat at a table near the front entrance. Sanaya glanced at her and sighed, before taking a seat in a separate corner of the dining hall, praying not to run into Trent. Archer was near the dish room engaged in a serious conversation with a group of Guardians when she sensed the familiar and undeniable energy signature of none other than King. Congo was behind him, instructing him on what to do and where to go. It was obvious King must have sensed her too because he spun around, searching the sea of students frantically and when he spotted her, a slight grin spread across his face. She tried not to show her own excitement, but the sight of the handsome young man made her heart flutter. Maya must have spotted him too because she could not keep her eyes off of him as he sauntered passed her and took a seat at the table with Sanaya.

Sanaya could feel her friend's eyes on her, but she chose to ignore it. Maya was not in a place to ask questions and expect answers since they technically were not speaking.

She swallowed thickly as King's own masculine aroma combined with Mountain Spring soap entered her nostrils. Damn he smelled good.

"Hi…" He said, his eyes drinking her in, never leaving her face.

"Hi…" She replied. She noticed the moment he took a seat; Archer, Congo, Tia and Eve were all glaring in their direction as if they were plotting some sort of conspiracy.

"So you're the girl in my head," King continued.

God, he is even better looking this close…Sanaya thought..

~ 86 ~

"Sorry about that," she began, forcing herself to take a bite of her pancake. "My powers are…strengthening and it just sort of happened."

"No, it's cool ma. I'm just used to being up in everyone else's head instead of someone being in mine, ya feel me?" Even his voice was liquid velvet, offering a soothing effect that made her limbs feel like jelly.

"Same here. Before I was found, I was the only one who could hear, see and smell everything that was going on around me, including things that moved in the dark-"

"When did you? How did you?"

"My dad was turned into a vampire and decided to bring home the good news to his family. That is the night that I learned that there is a lot more to me than what I knew before."

Taking a bite of his own food which included strips of bacon and scrambled eggs, he continued with his line of questioning. "Well obviously there is definitely a lot more to you. What are you a princess or something? They got you under heavy protection."

"There is a lot going on around here otherwise, I wouldn't be under this much supervision."

"Who did you piss off? The Pope?" He chuckled while taking in another bite.

"No. A master vampire."

He stopped chewing.

"So I take it even though you are new, you know the deal on that type of entity right?"

"I know a little something. You're not a Guardian are you? You're something special huh?"

She cringed when he said "special". She felt everything else but that.

"I wouldn't say all of that, but I am what I am apparently, and lots of people would think of me as anything but."

He smiled at her. "Nah, they just hatin'. I didn't pick up anything but special from you, and I'm good at reading people. You ain't no ordinary bit-lady. Lady…excuse me, I.."

"No, it's alright. I get what you are saying."

"Time to go kids," came an unhappy voice from behind.

Sanaya's head whipped around to meet the disapproving stare of Archer. She hesitantly grabbed her plate, not ready to say goodbye to the handsome stranger. "See you around?"

Before he could open his mouth in response, Congo answered for him. "He does not have idle time to spare dear Slayer. Just like you, he has to acclimate himself to his new home and receive the appropriate training otherwise he cannot stay within the walls of The Academy."

King's eyes blazed with defiance, and she could sense Archer's tension, she quickly sent King a message.

Chill…there is a lot going on. Everyone is on edge.

King grabbed his plate without looking at her. *When can I see you again?*

Classes maybe…

What about the courtyard?

When?

*Tonight…*King swung his back pack high above his shoulder.

Ok, tonight then.

Eve quickly stepped between Sanaya and King's personal exchange by ushering Sanaya behind Archer. Congo motioned for King to follow him, and as badly as she wanted to turn around and share one last glance in King's direction, Sanaya knew that it would be best if things between them were kept under wraps. But whatever it was that was growing between them, she simply could not suffocate the small spark that warmed her spirit. She felt his connection slip away as Eve walked beside her behind Archer, and wished like hell that for once in her life, she would be allowed to just be normal.

CHAPTER TWELVE

Crimson eyes created an eerie contrast in the surrounding darkness as Daemon watched Petronius's grin widen in satisfaction. Things were going as the leader of The Darkness Organization planned, while his own plans temporarily turned to dust.

"He's in!" Alex wheezed with rejoice. "I can't believe we managed to get the tainted spirit of a potential Guardian into The Academy!" The ancient vampire began to cough and sputter up black blood onto the cold, granite flooring of the bottom chambers in the first level of Hell where they would often convene. Little vampire bats rushed in a frenzied formation from the stalagmite rooftops for a taste of the regurgitated fluid, like hairy, airborne piranhas.

"That took a great deal of effort on our part to ensure that the strongest male guardian born would face adversities enough to break his spirit and weaken him to our side," Petronius replied, leaning forward on the black marble table and folding a tent with his long, deathly pale fingers. "Now that he is in, there is more work to be done. We must continue to put pressure on the backs of those obnoxious Guardians until the time comes for the Slayer to choose. What are your plans in all of this brother?" The oldest vampire of the three examined Daemon, his expression completely relaxed as if nothing was awry in the grand scheme of things.

Daemon took a sip of blood from the gold goblet. "My plans are always for the benefit of the empire Petronius," he articulated cautiously. He smoothed the lapels of his black business suit and crossed his legs. "What will you have me do?"

"I think you have enjoyed your stay in Rome for far too long brother," Petronius added coolly. "I need you to remain state side and with the remaining vampires we have at our disposal and whatever demon legions you have aligned yourself with, to put more pressure on the

Guardian teams here. There are not nearly enough of them to handle the carnage that we are capable of delivering."

"Are you insane?" Daemon quickly rose to his feet, his naturally midnight blue eyes blazing in the darkness. "If we draw too much attention to ourselves, we risk angelic intervention. There could be another war between our side and the forces of Light and to be honest, I look forward to surviving another millennium."

Petronius chuckled. "The war is indeed inevitable; however, I was just testing you brother. But we do need to make sacrifices for the benefit of the empire to draw more Guardian forces out of hiding, perhaps enough to enlist the aid from the Academy Guardians. Then I suggest we strategically place even more pressure on The Vatican, slowly tightening our grip until not only is the Slayer's spirit weakened, but so is the Guardian strength that surrounds her."

"That is brilliant!" Alex applauded as he struggled to balance himself upright on his feet.

"It is going to take all of us united to ensure the success of this plan," Petronius declared, his eyes never leaving Daemon's unreadable expression.

"It is indeed…" Daemon glanced at his perfectly manicured nails before continuing. "Well, if that is all you wanted to discuss, *brother*, I will return to the states as you requested. I've developed a craving for New Orleans cuisine anyways. Besides, I wanted to make it in enough time for Mardi Gras…"

"Very well then brother," Petronius nodded. "Until we meet again…"

Daemon dematerialized without another word from the cavernous pits of The Darkness Organization's power center while Petronius and Alex shared a knowing glance.

"Are you going to continue to allow him to play these childish games?" Alex wheezed, returning to his seat.

"It is better for him to hang himself Alex. He is going to have to face The Beast and explain why turn attempts are being made on Guardians when none of that had been sanctioned, and if The Beast doesn't kill him," Petronius' fangs lengthened as he growled, "we will."

∎∎

Eve took a seat on Sanaya's bed when Archer finally left. He was fuming the entire time about the new kid, King, making it crystal clear that the kid was not welcome anywhere near Sanaya for as long as he resided on campus. Sanaya stood there motionless as her Guardian mentor ranted and raved until he received a phone call that forced him to abandon Eve and Sanaya to their own devices. Sanaya attempted to busy herself by pulling out her history book with the hope of distracting herself with much needed studying even though the idea was futile.

Eve opened her mouth to speak, but Sanaya's silence forced her to take another approach. She waited until Sanaya was seated at the desk before cautiously approaching her. The young woman-child that she is carried a responsibility, which Eve did not want to fathom. Being a Guardian had enough of its own challenges. Hell, being a half breed vampire acting as a Guardian had been difficult. But her heart ached for the young woman that sat at the desk before her. This King kid could potentially be the worst thing that ever happened to her. Or, by Divine intervention, the very best. She gently placed her hand on Sanaya's shoulder, startling her. Sanaya looked up.

"Yes?" Sanaya asked, closing her book.

"Do you want to talk about it?" Eve asked carefully.

"Talk about what?"

"Everything…" Eve waited for Sanaya to respond, watching her intently. She watched her chest rise and fall, releasing some of the pent up anxiety that she more than likely lived with for most of her life. She smoothed away a few idle, stray hairs from her pretty almond brown face.

Such a lovely girl, Eve thought to herself.

"I don't know…everything just seems like too much right now…" Sanaya began with a sigh. "I'm tired of being on lockdown. I am tired of training, training and more training when other girls my age are allowed to go to the movies, hang out and just…have fun! I am tired of being hated for…I don't even know why the kids hate me!" Sanaya slammed her fist on the table, splintering it. "You see! That is not normal!" She screamed jumping up and freeze framing into the bathroom.

Eve tried to get to her before the door slammed shut, and she listened for the latch to lock, but when it hadn't, she gently eased her way through the door. Sanaya was crouched on the toilet with her face buried in her hands. Eve detected the soft scent of her tears which tightened the ache in her own heart.

"Do not cry Sanaya," she cooed as she kneeled beside her. "Please don't cry…"

"All I am is the fucking Slayer to you people…" Sanaya sobbed. "I was nothing to my own parents which made it difficult to even cry at their funerals." She wiped her face, revealing a pair of red rimmed eyes and sniffled. "I *hate it* here. My so called best friend is pissed off at me over a guy, a master vampire is tracking me; I'm afraid to go to sleep at night, and I…"

Eve pulled her into an embrace as another torrent of tears overwhelmed the young slayer, her pain a bottomless well that was dangerously close to consuming her spirit. Even the best warriors needed a moment to be human, and Sanaya was no exception.

"You are more than just a Slayer to us," Eve whispered into Sanaya's hair. "You are our hope… I did not mourn for my parents either. When I first arrived here no one would touch me with a ten-foot pole. All of them feared me because of what I am. But now…" Eve gently cradled Sanaya's face in her palms. "I proved all of them wrong, or right in some cases, but the fact remains, most of those people that had a problem accepting me would give their right hand to fight by me."

Instant understanding flowed between the two, and after a long moment, Sanaya barked out a laugh. "I hadn't cried since that night I watched my dad kill my mom," she said wiping her eyes.

"It's alright," Eve said soothingly. "You have been carrying that poison with you since you arrived. It's good that you got it out."

Eve tore off a handful of toilet paper from the roll and handed it to Sanaya before stepping back out into the bedroom to give the girl some much needed space. She still needed to ask her about what appeared to be blossoming between her and King, but the text message that came in through her phone told her the King conversation would have to wait another day.

Meeting in the war room. Sending Myra and Lois to cover you.

Eve sighed. There were still a couple of hours left before sundown, , and whatever Archer's plan of attack happened to be, she hoped that he had an effective plan in place. There was only a matter of time before the master sent out human helpers to lay siege on the Academy or worse. In her almost 200 years of existence, she learned a thing or two about master vampires and what they are capable of, and if Sanaya is indeed imbedded deeply into this particular vampire's radar, then they are going to need more than just a handful of Guardians to stop him. Plus, she could sense the limitless power of one of the ancient members of The Darkness Organization, and she was willing to bet her eyeteeth that he was behind this, which meant that The Guardians had a lot more to worry about. And, what the Guardians seemed to forget was that she, next to Sanaya was their secret weapon into the vampire world. Experience with killing vampires was one thing, but actually being one of them was another.

Sanaya returned to her desk to finish her studies, her mood apparently lifted placing her in a much clearer space, and without a word, Eve gently closed the door so as not to disturb her. She should be fine with the two younger Guardians, at least until she gets back from the meeting. Myra and Lois were experienced Guardians, and even though their specialty did not reside in all things vampire, they would know what to do, especially if the master attempted another mind lock with the Slayer before the sun sets. Myra, an expert in protection wards and all things dreamscape should be able to handle the situation. Massaging her temples, Eve tried to relax, unsure of where all of the sudden tension was coming from when she detected the presence of Lois and Myra outside of the door.

The two blondes greeted her warmly, with Myra, the shorter of the two, taking a seat on the sectional in the living area.

"So where is she?" She asked excitedly, her blue eyes wide with enthusiasm.

"She is in the room studying. For now, just give her some space. She has had a rough few days."

Lois and Myra nodded as Eve headed out the door. Despite her understanding that Sanaya was left in the care of good hands, the anxiety of leaving the Slayer alone would not dissipate.

CHAPTER THIRTEEN

Sanaya closed her book the moment Eve left and checked her phone to find that there were a dozen text messages from Maya, apologizing profusely for her behavior; and at least three from Trent wanting to know if she was ok. She responded to Maya's text, figuring that Maya was busy with her own studies when her best friend surprised her with an immediate follow up call.

" Naya, I am so sorry," She began, sounding sincere.

"It's cool…" Sanaya replied, taking a seat on the edge of the bed. "I hope you are over it."

"I don't know what came over me.I just, like him so much."

"But Maya," Sanaya pleaded. "You don't even know him. I mean, yeah he is fine and everything but sheeesh…"

"Like I said, I am sorry…"

"Well, you are forgiven…just don't lose your head over a guy again. I wouldn't do you like that."

"I know you wouldn't," Maya said softly. "I just wanted him to see me the way that everyone else sees you…"

Maya's last comment sent a pang of pain right in the center of Sanaya's chest. Her best friend, her sister just revealed that she felt trapped in her shadow and for that, Sanaya couldn't stay mad at her. Besides, she had much bigger issues to contend with, but before moving on to that, she had to let Maya know her own truth as well.

"Maya, you are special just because you are you. That's it. It has nothing to do with your gifts or what people may think your future will hold. You are just you. Trent only likes me because of *what* I am, not who I am, just like everyone else here at this school…"

"I didn't realize that-"

"No you didn't. But how could you?"

When Maya did not immediately respond, Sanaya decided it was just time to let it go. Maya was still her friend regardless. Things were tense around The Academy.

"So, who is the new guy that sat at the table with you this morning?" Maya prodded.

"Oh, Maaaaayyyaaa, his name is King and-"

"You like him!" Maya squealed over the phone, making Sanaya cringe.

"Shhhhh! Don't mention anything about that out loud. I don't think the Guardians like him too much and…"

Sanaya then gave her friend the rundown on her encounters with the new potential Guardian, negating to mention that they were supposed to meet at the Courtyard tonight at midnight. Some things were just too private and too special for even a BFF to know about.

"Damn girl," Maya said when she was finished. "I saw you two together and he looked like he was way into you…"

"I know. He is…" Sanaya gushed. She checked the clock and she had a few more hours before she made her escape. She knew the head Guardians would be out hunting tonight, so manipulating the two that were supposed to be watching her should be a breeze, or at least that is what she figured.

"But check it, I got some interesting news to share with you," Maya added, interrupting her thoughts.

"What is it?"

"I overheard Tia talking to that Guardian brother, Andre, about three of the students that have gone missing," Maya said quickly. "You see,

Elizabeth is one of the few here that are the least gifted and her antics along with the crap she pulled with you the other day has landed her in big trouble with her family. Her father is threatening to pull her out of the school because he feels that she has been an embarrassment to the family name, so now she is desperate. Elizabeth wants to be a Guardian. Her whole future is depending on it, so she sent out three of her flunkies on a mission to dig up some information about the vampire activity taking place around the school for them to bring it back to her so *she* can try to do something about it and make herself look good in front of The Academy."

"That is so effing stupid of her! And her flunkies! They're that stupid to risk their lives just to make her look good?" Sanaya exclaimed in disbelief.

"Naya, you forgot Elizabeth has money and so she probably promised them that if they do this for her, she would reward them with some cash or something…you know she likes to floss her parents' wealth to the rest of us who pretty much have nowhere else to go outside of The Academy."

"But how did they get out? This place has pretty much been on lock down."

"The Guardians are stretched too thin here. Most of them are away on secret missions, while the rest are divided between hunting the master, guarding the school and protecting you. Plus, we've got some strong seers on this campus, and I'm willing to bet that one of Elizabeth's flunkies were strong enough to temporarily block the Guardians from knowing their whereabouts until it was too late."

Sanaya didn't hesitate when she said, "Maya, we gotta do something. I can't live like this."

"I know but what? They are never going to let us fight until they think we are ready," Maya added pensively.

"Well Maya, we have to prove to them that we don't have time."

They wrapped up their conversation with a plan Sanaya could only hope would work, and then checked the time again. Two more hours.

She didn't care about what she had to do to make it to the courtyard. Maya had given her an idea she hadn't even considered. She was a strong telepath. Not strong enough to break Archer's blocks nor set up her own blocks against him; she was almost as strong as Eve, but still needed a ways to go. She gently sent out a mental probe to test the new Guardian's resistance to her, and when she found none, she knew these Guardians had special skills, but unfortunately was lacking in the Seer department. She could get around them easily.

Besides, if the campus was supposed to be a fortress, then what could possibly go wrong?

▪▪

Two hours later

King waited patiently underneath the Willow tree in the courtyard, hoping that Sanaya had managed to get away from her caretakers. He just needed a moment with her. Just one. Her presence was enough to make sense of all the stuff that had gone terribly wrong in his world. It wasn't easy getting passed Congo, however when the Guardian giant left to attend an important meeting, he used that as his opportunity to escape, slipping out of his room with ease and taking the back stairs to circumvent the parking lot, cutting across a narrow path that led to the courtyard. He made sure to dress in all black attire which included sweats and a hoodie, but at some he figured, if he was going to get caught it was going to happen regardless. Just about every person who attended or worked for this school had special abilities without actually having to see him in the dark.

Leaning against the trunk of the tree, he checked the phone Congo gave him. It was two after midnight. He knew she would come. There was determination in her promise that she would be there. The night stood still, and he listened in the surrounding darkness for any signs of movement. There was none, other than the gentle breeze that rustled the Willows hanging branches. After another few minutes, he sensed the familiar energy signature of Sanaya approaching. Like him, she sported the all black look with her perfectly fitted sweats and thin jacket. She looked around anxiously, her guard obviously up and the moment her eyes met his, a slow smile crept along her pretty face.

"Hey pretty girl," He greeted. "You made it. I thought the Guardians had you on a tight lock down."

She looked away, still smiling. "I have my ways of getting around those things." The truth was, she temporarily mind stunned the Guardians so she could slip out. They had no idea what hit them. After that, she crawled through a nearby vent in the hall before exiting out of the building, and making sure to stick to the shadows. When Archer discovers what she'd done, she knew she was in big trouble.

"Looks like you had little trouble making your escape," She said inching closer to him.

"I can take care of myself," He replied with a grin.

They stood in awkward silence, Sanaya unsure of what else to say. Instead, she moved in closer, until she stood just inches away from him.

"So where are you from?" She asked finally, folding her arms across her chest.

"Georgia. You?"

"Los Angeles."

"So tell me about this…"

He didn't get a chance to finish his sentence when Sanaya sensed the presence of something "otherly" hidden in the shadows, watching them. Raising her finger to her lips, motioning him to remain silent, she stretched out her senses. Her skin began to prickle, her body tensed and she instinctively took a protective position in front of King.

"What is…?"

"Shhhhh…" She silenced him again, so she could listen. This school was supposed to be a fortress: a bastion against the levels of darkness. The school was built on hallowed ground, blessed by every Pope known to man. Where are the Guardians? The all too familiar scent of sulfur caused bile to build up in her throat. Her heart rate increased, fueling her body with adrenaline. Tuning her ears into the surrounding darkness, she heard the soft patter of feet against the pavement off in the distance, closing in. Vampire. A vampire was on the campus!

She snatched a thick branch off of her favorite tree, snapping it in half, mumbling her own prayer over it, creating her own version of a stake. King stood behind her and did the same thing.

The entity was closing in at full speed, and Sanaya could sense its thirst. Female. Fresh turn. Sanaya's mental probe determined a familiarity with the vampire.No. This couldn't be…

Sanaya didn't have time to finish the thought when Halo appeared, looking half crazed and enraged. Her once beautiful brown skin had an ashen grey tinge to it. She now sported fangs, her slanted eyes now glowed a deep crimson. Her clothes were tattered and ripped, and the gaping wound from where she'd been bitten had yet to heal.

"What the fuck?" King shouted, while Sanaya faced off with Halo.

"Pretty Slayer," Halo growled. "The Master wants you alive but do not make me violate his orders by killing you."

Sanaya circled the vampire/former Guardian, her stake held firmly in her grip.

"Tell your Guardians to call off their hunt, otherwise more students will join his army."

"Who did this to you Halo?" Sanaya demanded. "Tell me the Master's name."

Halo smiled, exposing her freshly formed, blood dripped fangs. Sanaya shuddered. Halo had fed and the only thing she could hope was that it was not from any one of the students. Enraged, Sanaya launched a series of hard punches inn Halo's direction, knocking the vampire back. However, Halo at one point was one of the strongest Guardians at The Academy and it was not long before she had the upper hand, landing a hard swing into Sanaya's jaw. Sanaya doubled back but would not give up, and when Halo launched into the air in her direction, Sanaya met her with a hard kick to the chest. King tried to assist by landing a couple of punches of his own, however Halo managed to grab him by his hoodie and sent him flying across the courtyard where he crashed into a nearby bench, his body bounced twice before hitting the grass.

Guardians came rushing out, armed with stakes, cross bows and specially calibrated guns with silver bullets, while Sanaya fought Halo with everything she had. She barely missed a swipe from Halo's talons when she hit her with another punch to the jaw.

"I can't get a clear shot!" She heard one of the Guardians yell.

"Sanaya!" Came Eve's voice.

She could hear the Guardians calling for her, but it was too late. This was her kill. Halo lunged for her again, and this time she ended up on the ground, with Halo's fangs just inches above her neck.

"Ronan will just have to understand," Halo hissed.

Eve reached her before the other Guardians and yanked Halo by the neck, forcing her off her. Sanaya was on her feet instantly, brandishing her stake and made another run for Halo.

"Sanaya nooooo!" Archer screamed as Sanaya plunged the stake deep into Halo's chest cavity. However, instead of turning into ash, Halo was on the ground, spewing up blood, her muscles spasming. Sanaya went for her again when she was pulled back by Eve and Congo.

"Why won't you die!" Sanaya screamed as she struggled against Congo and Eve's hold.

"Easy sweetheart," Congo said soothingly. "You did good. Real good."

At least a dozen Guardians surrounded Halo, weapons drawn. The vampire thrashed about violently, sending a high pitched scream into the night air.

"How the hell did she cross our barriers man?" Another Guardian demanded.

"Take her inside," Archer commanded grimly, motioning towards Sanaya.

"Come on honey," Eve said gently, ushering Sanaya and Congo towards the main building.

Sanaya calmed enough to allow herself to be escorted from the violent scene. As her senses normalized, she felt the soul chilling caress brush across her exposed shoulder. She tensed, recognizing immediately the invisible culprit. She clenched her jaws shut. The Guardians were already in over their heads.

"I know you felt him," Eve whispered to her as they approached the steps. "He is close."

"Who is close?" Congo demanded.

"The Master," Eve replied.

Congo cursed as Eve continued. "He won't breach the school. Something or someone is holding him back. He has already had a taste of our Slayer and the knowledge that she is close is driving him to the point of madness. Halo was sent." She inhaled deeply, fighting back tears. "Halo was sent to weaken our resolve and our defenses. But, the fact that she didn't turn to ash even with the stake in her chest means that she wasn't supposed to turn. She won't die until we put the master that killed her down."

The three of them said nothing more once they entered the multistory building. Sanaya's thoughts went to King, and from what she could determine based on her mental survey of the scene, he was unconscious and being loaded onto a stretcher. She sensed his pulse, which to her was a good sign. Again another mistake. She should have taken him away and ran for it instead.

They walked down a corridor with hanging portraits of the fallen Slayers that had come before her, and she took her time, taking each one of them in. All of them, female. All of them, being called to serve a higher purpose of defending humanity from the Darkness that threatened to devour and destroy everything in its wake. They rounded a corner before they ended up in the small chapel that was built specifically for the school.

"It seems this is the safest place," Congo murmured, closing the double doors behind him.

"We should move some of the students here and perhaps take the rest to the other side of The Vatican. The Archbishop is sending over his assassins to help guard…"

"How did a vampire breach our grounds?" Sanaya asked finally, drawing the attention of both Guardians.

"I don't know young one," Congo confessed. "But I'm sure Archer will have some answers."

"Do you have anything you'd like to tell us Sanaya?" Eve asked, while Sanaya took a seat on one of the pews.

"Like why you were outside with my charge after midnight?" Congo added, crossing his arms.

Sanaya lowered her gaze to her feet and silently wished that she could be anywhere in the world instead of this chapel in front of these inquiring Guardians. Some things were just too special to discuss or defend. Whatever this was between herself and King, there were no words to accurately describe. Neither of these Guardians would understand and there was no way she was revealing her true feelings.

"Both of us heard something." She knew the lie was a weak one but she didn't care.

"Y'all heard something?" Congo repeated in disbelief. "And y'all just thought you are that bad ass to take care of it yourselves, huh?" He shook his head. "You know, Slayer or not I expected better from you Sanaya. The boy is unconscious and even though I am sure that he will be alright but still. He is a strong potential Guardian, but even he isn't immune to vampire or demon bites. He hasn't even begun his formal training. Hell, you ain't even finished with yours!" Congo slammed his heavy fist onto a nearby table, rattling it.

"Eve, talk to her," Congo mumbled, walking away. "Because I can't. This job has become too stressful for me and the last thing I want to deal with is two teenagers going on a midnight romantic stroll believing that they can take care of themselves." Congo stormed out, leaving the two of them alone.

"I'm sorry..." Sanaya whispered through unshed tears.

"I know you are desperate to spread your wings," Eve said gently. "But just like the eagle that spreads its wings against the wind, even he had to wait until his feathers for flight were ready. The eagle must learn to fly not just against the flow of a gentle breeze, but above and through raging storms. And eagles, do not leave the nest until they are ready…until their wings are fully developed. Yours are barely forming and you will have plenty of time to test them out when they are ready. Understand?"

Sanaya nodded.

"And one more thing Sanaya," Eve added. "I am not here to tell you what to do, let alone who you should be attracted to, but I would take a step away from King for a while. That young man is fresh out of a life of darkness, using his precious gifts for self-gain and could very well be a marker for The Darkness. We don't know yet. Trent, same thing. These young men were pulled from the clutches of darkness and were well on their way to becoming powerful agents of their cause and they didn't even know it. They have a lot to learn about themselves here, so before you go there in your mind with him, give him some space to choose which side he is on. The last thing I want for you to experience is to have to put a stake in the heart of someone who carries yours in the palm of his hand." Eve left Sanaya alone on the pews facing the alter with the glass portrait of the Virgin Mary sitting high above the pulpit, while she stepped outside to speak with another Guardian. Halo's screams could still be heard somewhere within the protective walls of the campus, and Sanaya wondered what the other students may be thinking.

Not that it mattered. No one but the Virgin herself knew that she wished she could disappear into a black box and scream.

CHAPTER FOURTEEN

The next morning was plagued with an endlessly long sermon to the hundred and some odd students about responsibility, honor and all of the other attributes that made a Guardian. Sanaya sat next to Maya towards the front, and tried to pay attention to what Archer was saying to her peers. However, the events from last night still haunted her. In lieu of the missing students, it had been decided by The Vatican to provide students the opportunity to return home temporarily until the threat was handled. Those that decided to go home (or had homes to return to) would be escorted home by Guardian volunteers, and for those who stayed had to deal with being under complete lock down until further notice. No one was to leave their rooms when the sun set and were not permitted to leave for class until later on in the morning when the sun was at its highest.

Sanaya still had a few bruises from the night before including a swollen jaw and a sprained hand, but instead of fear or hatred that she usually received from the other students, respect glimmered in their eyes when she walked by. King was ok, and he secretly hit up her mental inbox letting her know along with a few choice words of praise in her direction. She tried not to show it, but for the first time she felt pretty damned good about herself. Word must have spread via King how she faced off fearlessly with Halo and how it took a couple of Guardians to pull her off. That and the fact that Elizabeth was nowhere around to fan the fire of hate in her direction.

After Archer finished his speech, all classes were cancelled for the day, and even though she was technically on "punishment", courtesy of Archer and Eve, Maya was welcomed back into her room as the exception to her penance for mind stunning Guardians and sneaking out. When the speech was over, the students were dismissed in groups, with Sanaya's group being the last to leave. King walked passed her, pretending to have not seen her but connecting with her mentally as always.

Hey beautiful, he shot to her as he walked ahead of another student

Hey and thanks... She tried hard to act like she was busy with her phone, but the flush of her cheeks gave it away.

I'll call you later, he promised, referring to their private form of communication.

Archer caught Sanaya's starry eyed gaze and scowled. She straightened in her seat, while Maya chuckled.

"Man, Archer is going to send you to Antarctica if you don't learn how to play it cool," She teased.

"I know but I can't help it," Sanaya giggled.

"Girl he is all inside your head isn't he?" Maya asked.

Before Sanaya could respond, Archer motioned for them to get up so they can be escorted to their dorms.

As the two of them walked shoulder to shoulder, Maya nudged Sanaya and began whispering in hushed tones.

"You ever hear of the Guardian Mate Bond?" she asked Sanaya who just glanced at her with confusion.

"No, what is that?"

"I think that is why Archer and Eve are about to have a cow about you and King," Maya said slowly.

"I don't even know what that is but I sincerely doubt it because I barely know the guy to form any type of bond."

"I read about it during health class. Guardians form bonds with each other that are different from regular human relationships."

"Well what is it?" Sanaya asked urgently. She turned around to see if anyone was watching them and sure enough, Archer was several steps behind them and Eve was now in the front.

"A Guardian Mate Bond is this special connection formed when two Guardians are destined to be together. It is supposed to be this unexplainable connection between two Guardians that links them as soul mates. I think they sense one forming between you two and they don't know what to do…"

"Maya that is crazy!" Sanaya protested even though a part of Maya's statement made sense to her.

"Think about it. You two mind locked with one another before meeting in person. You said so yourself you couldn't figure out how you did it."

"Yeah but…"

"You broke a rule for him last night and you never break rules, unless you're fighting. And I am still a little pissed that you didn't tell me that was what you were going to do but hey, I forgive you."

"I still don't know Maya…"

"It really doesn't sound so crazy at all. It actually makes sense. I bet he is taking up space all in your head. Had he been a regular crush, Archer wouldn't even care. But again, you broke rules, serious ones at that and so, yup, Archer is going to try his best to keep the two of you apart." Maya started to chuckle, and Sanaya quickened her pace.

"And what about you and Trent?" Sanaya huffed as her friend struggled to keep up.

"I'm not getting my hopes up on him. He barely notices me." Maya said sadly.

Sanaya wrapped her arm around her BFF and said, "Girl, he will eventually recognize your fabulous glory. They all do."

Maya laughed. "I hope so. He has no idea what he is missing out on."

- -

Daemon's expression remained calm as his messenger informed him of the latest news transpiring at The Academy. Ronan, once again had acted prematurely and out of order and for that, there would be redress. Unfortunately, he was stuck in Louisiana for the time being per Petronius orders, but he would be on his way to Rome soon. The good news is that in Ronan's haste to claim the Slayer, it was discovered that the grounds weren't so protected after all but then again, with the Guardian being an unsanctioned turn, her guardian blood still permitted entry despite her condition. There was no way to know until he saw for himself that vampires could cross the supposed hallowed ground. As a matter of fact, he had an appointment with the current Pope later on in the week to discuss weakening some of those barriers…The Catholic Church was no longer what it used to be and it had taken him many centuries to weaken their resolve.

The world didn't need any more slayers-not even for the benefit of a day walker; and he would see to it that the Slayer did not reach maturity. Petronius wasn't the only one with plans for the girl's twenty first birthday. No. He had his own plans. The Beast would be appeased either way, and with the girl out of the way and the next Slayer possibly not scheduled for birth for another thousand years. In the meantime, he would be free to unleash his demon legions upon mankind; overthrow Petronius and Alex; and bring the world to its knees. And with the rare occurrences of angelic intervention, humanity was ripe and ready for the picking.

Daemon reclined into his leather seating and motioned for the hooded figure that stood before him to go on its way. The creature bowed and then disappeared into mist. Daemon checked his watch, realizing that the sun would set soon. Louisiana was beautiful at night, and tonight he would feed well.

The dining hall was unusually quiet when Sanaya entered, accompanied by Maya, Eve, Tia Archer and a couple of other Guardians. *This is starting to get really, really old*, Sanaya thought to herself as she grabbed a tray and made her way to an empty table. King was nowhere in sight, and neither was Congo. However, Trent had just walked in accompanied by Lois and Myra and spotted her and Maya as they took a seat. He made a beeline for his tray, dumping anything and everything on his plates before pulling up a seat next to Maya.

"Wassup yall," He said, winking at Sanaya.

Sanaya sighed, while Maya looked away.

"Hey Trent," Sanaya said, with a sudden loss of appetite.

Trent flashed both of them a toothy, perfect grin. "Man, yall know that new kid King?" He began, his eyes still focused on Sanaya. "I know you know him-and you need to let ol' boy know you are spoken for."

"Excuse me?" Sanaya snapped, dropping her fork onto her plate. "Uh, no I am not. Last I checked I was single."

"Well that day changed when I showed up," Trent grinned, taking a bite of his burger.

"I don't think so-"

"So what did King say?" Maya interjected, desperate to change the subject.

"Yoooooo, he got the chance to see my girl here in action," Trent bragged.

Sanaya and Maya both cringed the moment he said "my girl", but he didn't seem to notice. He just kept right on talking.

"He said that you had this crazy ass look in your eyes and…"

All of sudden, Sanaya could not hear a word that was coming out of Trent's mouth. She felt his presence before he appeared through the door. Her heart rate began to race as soon as his handsome, dark face appeared through the doorway accompanied with Congo. Smooth chocolate skin, an athletic body as evidence from playing a variety of sports. His black V-neck did little to mask the well-defined abs and chiseled pecks. Without even looking at her he sent a mental embrace her way, sending a chill down her spine. His long, intricately twisted dreads were pulled back away from his face. How she'd love to run her fingers through his-

"Sanaya! Girl, snap out of it," Maya barked with a laugh. "Earth to Naya…earth to Naya…"

"What? Huh?" Sanaya said shaking her head and trying to pretend like she was preoccupied with her food.

"Damn ma, you just gon' play me like that?" Trent remarked, his tone with a bit of bite to it than usual.

"Play who?" Came the voice she could not get out of her head, even if she tried. "Can I sit down?"

Sanaya was all too thrilled to answer. Her response was her moving her tray over to make room for his. As he sat down, Sanaya and Maya shared a glance, both masking huge smirks that were threatening to reveal themselves.

"Look at you girl," Maya squealed in her head. *"You can't even contain yourself."*

"Shut up. I can't help it-"

"Ay dog," Trent said, his eyes focused on King. "This table is taken."

King glanced over at Sanaya and inched closer to her. "Doesn't look like it from here. I was invited." And to add insult to injury, King swung his arm over Sanaya's shoulders, his glare never leaving Trent's. *Feeling froggish…*His eyes told Trent. *Jump then.*

Trent stood up to meet his challenge, but when it was clear that their table had full Guardian attention, he grabbed his tray to leave. "You wanna roll with me Maya?" He asked, his gaze completely focused on Maya's surprised glance.

"Uh, yeah sure," she said taking the hint. "See you at the dorm Naya?"

"Yeah." The two girls held each other's stares, both silently squealing for joy, when Maya turned around and followed Trent to another table.

King didn't hesitate to express his dislike for Trent. "What's up with you and that clown? Let me know before I involve myself in something I shouldn't."

"Nothing is up. Trent has only been here maybe a day or two longer than you. He likes me or he did like me but that is about it," she said coolly.

"And your friend? Is she cool or nah?"

"Maya? She's been my best friend since I arrived here. She's always had my back. She just has a thing for Trent."

"Aight. Cool." King raised his glass and took several long gulps of his lemonade, while Sanaya watched.

"I'm glad you are ok," she said quietly.

He set his glass down and faced her, smiling. "No. I'm glad you are ok, girl. You were straight gangsta with that vamp! I ain't neva met a shawty as bad as you. That's what they taught you here?"

When she nodded, he continued. "Like for real for real…you ain't even need my help. You fought like a pro."

"Thanks King."

"I see why they keep twenty four hour guard over you…and these suckas in this school are fools for not wanting to team up with you. Just know that I am your number one fan and…" He looked around and when he saw the hard stare coming from Archer, he switched over to telepathy.

And I wanna know you…like get to know you.

She raised her eyebrows so high, she thought she felt her entire face lift. *Like how?*

Be your homie/boyfriend/friend type deal-but not now. I want to know you Sanaya.

If she was of fairer skin, her face would be bright red right now. *I want to get to know you too King.*

I don't even know you but I feel like I've been knowing you all my life…

I know, it's crazy…I don't even have to grant you permission to get inside my head. Usually, it's like someone knocking on the door, but with you, you just waltz right in.

Just then, Tia stood in front of the hall and made the announcement that it was almost time for them to return to their dorms.

Quick, take out your phone and put my number in, she told him as she pulled out her own phone and unlocked it.

No more trips to the courtyard?

Sanaya looked up at him with a sheepish grin. *Afraid not. I've been grounded…*

King barked out a laugh, his eyes watering as he doubled over, trembling with amusement.

That is not funny! Sanaya protested, trying to sound outraged at his laughter. However, she had to admit it was pretty funny when she thought about it.

"I'm sorry shawty," He continued to chuckle with amusement. "But you? A vampire slayer is grounded? That just doesn't sound right. But I get it. They put my ass under lock down too…"

Sanaya noticed Archer heading in her direction and quickly snatched his phone and locked her number in. King followed suit and by the time she was sliding her phone back in her pocket, Archer was at their table telling her it was time for her to go. The Guardian didn't even acknowledge King's presence, while he waited for Sanaya to gather her things, but it didn't matter. She looked at him, her eyes read: *Call me tonight. I will be up.*

King nodded and when Archer turned his back, he quickly took Sanaya's hand in his and placed a gentle kiss across her bruised knuckles. When she gasped, Archer turned around and glared at both of them.

"I hope that makes it better," King said, undeterred by Archer.

"It does," Sanaya replied, her palm still in his hand.

"That's it you two," Archer growled. "Congo, come get Romeo while I escort Juliet to her room where she will not be allowed outside of…ever."

A few students walked by, snickering as Sanaya lowered her gaze in embarrassment.

"Come on Romeo," Congo mumbled as he took King's tray and led them through the front exit.

Sanaya followed Archer as he collected Maya and Trent. Trent didn't bother looking in her direction, but she didn't care, and when she and

~ 116 ~

Maya were finally alone in the room they now shared, she couldn't wait to close the door to give her best friend all of the details.

"Sanaya," Maya chirped as she took a seat on the floor. "Tell me everything."

▪▪

CHAPTER FIFTEEN

Eve sat in the other room trying to give the girls their privacy while Archer sat across from her on the love seat with his legs spread, balancing his elbows with his knees, and head down low in defeat.

"What am I going to do?" He sighed.

"About what?" Eve asked, even though she knew exactly what he was talking about.

"Our Slayer...she seems to be going through these extreme phases of bloodlust which according to the Highers up, in their archives is not supposed to happen for another three years."

"Well, she is different. She is supposed to be the strongest ever born-"

"And then there is this King character. Did you see that look in her eyes whenever she's near him?"

"Yes...I did."

"And then what makes things worse is both of them are strong enough to communicate telepathically. Her best friend can't even do that yet- not unless she is communicating with someone stronger than her-"

"That means that it has begun..." Now it was Eve's turn to sigh.

"She's too young for that type of bond!" Archer exclaimed.

"Shhhhh...keep your voice down. She will hear you," Eve pleaded.

"And on top of everything else, we have a horny master that is after her-"

"But think about it...Mate Bonds, if strong enough can block out any unwanted mind locks, especially vampire. If what I think is happening betwixt the two of them is indeed happening, her bond to King can keep her safe until we figure out a way to kill the master that hunts her."

"I don't want to run the risk of that bond leading to other results either if you know what I'm saying…"

"I do understand, but as long as we don't give them any room for that type of activity she will be fine…"

"The kid is bad news Eve. Bad. I don't trust him. He was supposed to be a Guardian-"

"And he still is but we have to teach him. We failed him before, so it is not his fault that he is the way that he is. But, Sanaya may be the bridge to get through to him. You walked the path of the dark side before-"

"But there is something about him that I can't put my finger on-"

"Give him a chance Archer. She's seventeen-"

"And he's nineteen-"

"Not much difference…besides, the age of consent laws are different out here anyways if it came down to it-which it won't."

"If he breaks her heart I will kill him myself," Archer said flatly.

"So the Darkness could claim your soul and torture you forever?"

"I'm just saying-"

"And I'm just saying…give him a chance. Besides, the girl has not had much happiness since she arrived, and probably long before that."

Archer leaned back against the couch in defeat. "I hate it when you're right. You know that?"

Eve slid from her side of the room and crawled into his lap, wrapping her arms around his neck. "But you love it when I tell you things you already know. It means we are on the same page."

She pressed her mouth against his, and he welcomed her in. She understood his concern with the Mate bond, because as complicated as their relationship could be, she knew all too well what it meant. But with age comes the wisdom in finding peace in the fact that something great was at work and even if they had no clue what to do about it, understanding would happen in time. They would just have to wait and see.

It wasn't even an hour after Sanaya spilled the beans on what went on with King and Maya had showered and prepared for bed when her best friend was passed out sleep on one end of the bed. Sanaya decided to do the same by jumping in the steaming hot shower, shampooing and conditioning her hair, before climbing into bed. When she was settled in, her phone rang with King's number showing up as the caller. Her palms shook with excitement as she struggled to answer the phone without dropping it.

"Hello?" She whispered into the receiver as she fell back onto the pillow.

"Hi beautiful," came King's silky voice. "Did I wake you or something?"

"No, no it's fine. I just hopped in the bed."

"Without me?"

"Huh? Oh uh-"

"I'm just teasing you boo. You're not going to get in trouble are you?"

"For what? Talking on the phone?"

"No. For talking to me."

"Even if I did, it wouldn't matter…"

"Why?"

"Because I like talking to you. I like the sound of your voice…" She thought she could hear him smiling over the phone.

"I like talking to you too beautiful." And that was it, the floodgates crumbled and before they knew it, both were on the phone until the sun's rays threatened to peek over the horizon. They laughed and talked about everything they could think of, including Sanaya's dysfunctional parents and King's life on the streets and his now former girlfriend LaQuanda.

"Do you miss her?" Sanaya found herself asking, secretly hating the fact that another girl had some claim to this young Guardian that was slowly but surely stealing her heart.

"Nah. She was cool people. She took me in when I had nowhere to go. She was loyal, but I always knew she wasn't the one."

"How did you know?"

She felt him shrug. "I just knew…and then you came along and proved me right."

Sanaya glanced out of the window, realizing that she'd been up all night. "King…"

"Yeah I know I gotta let you go. We've been up all night.."

"I just-"

"I don't want to let you go," they both said simultaneously. Sanaya laughed.

"Well thank God classes are cancelled again today," she said with a yawn.

"I know right? Well, get some sleep beautiful. I probably will miss breakfast, so maybe I will sit with you at lunch?" When she yawned again he chuckled. "Never mind, make that dinner."

"I will be at lunch…"

"Alright then Sanaya, goodnight."

"Goodnight."

Sanaya hung up the phone and turned around to face Maya who'd been awake for quite some time and smiled.

"I take it you're not going to breakfast," she said with a smirk.

Sanaya rolled over onto her side and smiled. "No. But I will see you at lunch."

Sanaya was surprised that the Guardians had allowed her to sleep in until lunch time. But, classes were cancelled until further notice due to The Vatican calling every available Guardian to action-including the older Guardians who were supposed to be "retired" from the field. There was still no news as to what happened to the missing students, and despite the few setbacks to her plan, Sanaya was determined to find out. Taking a seat at their favorite table by the back exit door, Sanaya sensed a familiar presence in the background staring at her. She didn't have to turn around to know that her arch nemesis had somehow weaseled her way back into the school.

"I guess the she-wolf is back huh?" Maya asked taking a seat.

"I guess so…as long as she doesn't start any shit," Sanaya sighed. After having only four hours of sleep, every bone in her body felt like she'd been in a fight. She arched her back to stretch her spine, relishing the feeling of bones and joints popping in the right places. She couldn't remember the last time she felt this exhausted. Yawning, she reached for her to dig into her lasagna when Maya's cursing made her whip her head around where Elizabeth and the remaining members of her pack sat; and lo and behold seated right next to her was Trent. Sanaya's eyes narrowed.

"Fucking traitor," Maya seethed, her large doe eyes blazing with anger…and hurt.

"Shoulda known dude would flip sides," Sanaya said looking away. "Now I know who not to have on my team."

~ 123 ~

Sanaya reached across the table and gently took Maya's clenched fist into hers. "He didn't deserve you in the first place," she said, knowing that that wasn't enough to cure the heartache Maya was going through.

"It's cool," Maya huffed. "It wasn't like he was interested in me anyway."

Sanaya watched from her mind's eye Elizabeth smiling and nestling in closer to Trent, and she secretly wished the Guardians would allow her just one moment to spar with her. Elizabeth would never again humiliate, isolate and bully other students again.

"Trent is an idiot," Sanaya heard herself say after a long pause. "I mean, think about it Maya…Trent's goal is to align himself with the most 'powerful'"-she said making the quotation marks, "person in the school. Ideally, he figured it might be us, considering what I am and what you are-"

"You mean you," Maya added sadly.

"No, us. Maya, you've got some serious mojo floating in your veins. You just have not been allowed to activate it yet. You're already a strong telepath-"

"But not strong enough to mind stun Guardians," Maya said with a chuckle.

"Not yet. Archer acknowledged it when he introduced us to Eve, remember?" When Maya nodded, she continued. "Anyways, think about it. Now he is aligning himself with Elizabeth and I am willing to bet it has everything to do with her money. That's it. Everyone here knows but refuses to admit that Elizabeth is actually the weakest link of the school which is why none of the Guardians have taken her out in the field yet. She has been here how long? Archer said as soon as you become stronger physically, he is taking you out on the field and that can be done in no time. Elizabeth has one more year I think before her training is done and then what? If Trent thinks that aligning himself with the queen bee of the school was the best decision to make, it sucks to be him. Especially if this campus ends up being under siege..." Sanaya didn't bother finishing her sentence. She didn't need to. Maya already knew what could possibly happen if the school ended up being attacked and there weren't enough Guardians.

The two ate in silence until it was time for them to go, and when Archer approached, standing next to the door, Sanaya heard Trent's voice yelling across the room for her and Maya's attention.

"Ay yo, Sanaya!" He shouted, wrapping his arm around Elizabeth, who actually blushed like a school girl.

Sanaya rolled her eyes, while Maya just kept her eyes on the door. Archer scowled.

"I swear I'm going to deck this kid," Sanaya overheard Archer mumbling to himself.

Sanaya grabbed Maya's arm and ushered her out of the door.

The trio-Archer, Sanaya and Maya- walked out onto the courtyard where Archer motioned for them to have a seat on the bench facing the dining hall. Neither girl spoke as they waited for the other Guardians to approach. Eve appeared, followed by Tia, Lois and Myra and a couple of other familiar Guardians, plus two additional individuals, dressed in the traditional Church assassin garb of black leather and trench coats. One of them-a woman in her early thirties-with porcelain skin, slanted eyes and petite feature; her silky straight jet black hair pulled away from her face into a single thick braid that hung well below the center of her back, kept one hand on the sheath of her blade. She regarded the other Guardians with little interest, while her partner, an older man probably in his early forties, his hazel brown eyes seemed to be focused primarily on Sanaya. His bronze skin glistened underneath the sun, and the raised four inch scar across his cheek became more apparent. Sanaya studied him, memorizing every detail from his long, thick mane that was also pulled away from his face in a single plait to the broad, heavily muscled shoulders. He as at least a foot taller than Archer who stood somewhere between 5'11" and 6'. Out of everyone that stood before her, this assassin had the strongest presence and she wondered what kind of abilities outside of fighting did he have at his disposal.

"I want you two to meet two very important people," Archer said interrupting her thoughts. "This is," Archer continued pointing to the male assassin. "Asim."

Asim bowed in her direction. "It is an honor and a pleasure to be of service to you young Slayer."

"And this is Tatsu," Archer said, as Tatsu offered her hand for Sanaya to accept.

Her grip was soft yet firm at the same time and upon contact, Sanaya detected a vague electric current coming off of this particular assassin. Tatsu smiled, acknowledging what Sanaya had sensed and Sanaya made a mental note to ask her about it later.

"These two will be your personal baby sitters until this whole thing blows over. We will be working with the church assassins round the clock to ensure the safety of the remaining students. Any questions?"

Yes she had questions. Many of them. But there was one question in particular that Sanaya needed answers for and one way or another Archer was going to tell her.

"Yes, Archer I do have one question," Sanaya began with a frown.

"Well shoot."

"Why didn't Halo die when I staked her? And how was she able to cross hallowed ground?"

She could feel Maya holding her breath and the other Guardians stared at her hard, while the two assassins smiled.

"First of all that was two questions. Secondly, that is classified information not meant for the ears of a first year student who is-"

"A slayer with a destiny to hunt evil," Sanaya continued defiantly. "That is what I am right?"

"I am not having this conversation with you Sanaya," Archer growled.

"Why?"

"Because one, I know you. Two, this is not Scooby Doo and the last thing I need is for you to drag Maya around, risking her life and yours-"

"If I might suggest something," Tatsu offered, facing Archer.

Archer faced her, his expression reflecting ever level of annoyance made known to mankind, but he kept his lips tightly sealed. The tension in his jaws were so tight, Sanaya noticed a muscle twitching and the vein that protrudes in the center of his forehead when he is upset, pulsated. Sanaya silently prayed that her Guardian did not spontaneously combust.

"I do not believe that it is within the interest of our slayer to be kept in the dark regarding such important matters. It might encourage her to react instead of act which could be harmful to her overall development. Besides, from what I heard she proved herself capable when the turned Guardian breeched the campus-"

"I am not having this discussion with you in front of the student who is in my charge!" Archer snapped, now returning his attentions on Sanaya. "And you, yes you are the Slayer. And yes you were born to hunt. Yes, you are probably the strongest one born since the beginning of time, but during this stage of the game, you are to listen to orders and not administer your own. You. Are. Not. Ready. End of story."

"But-"

"No buts Sanaya! You-"

"I can track the master Archer," Sanaya said firmly, her gaze unwavering.

"You were almost vamp snatched that night. Had Eve and I not dragged you off the street-"

"If you don't at least tell me what is going on more students are going to die," Sanaya whispered. Archer's hard glare under normal circumstances would have made her look away. However, things were different. She could feel it. The Church, as far as she knew never called upon its assassins unless there was a serious threat or some special mission that required skills of a particular specialty. Guardians usually took care of things for the most part. The fact that the assassins had been called to aid meant something much larger was at stake, and she was determined to find out what that is.

"And how do you know?" Archer replied softly.

"I feel it. And I know you sense it too…something isn't right."

Archer turned away an indicator to Sanaya that she had indeed made her point.

"How about this," Eve said trying to ease the tension that was now suffocating the group. "I think it is time that you start building your team. Why stand on ceremony and wait for her to choose? It is obvious the first person you would choose is Maya, and I'm afraid that were hindering your gifts. Classes have been cancelled until further notice, but for you Sanaya-and you too Maya, your training can continue. We have one strong Guardian potential that recently arrived-well two and we should add them to the group which would make three Guardians plus the Slayer. We need four more to give us the standard seven to make the protective formation around her, so that way, should whatever reason none of us are available-"

"I'm not liking this," Archer fumed. "Not at all."

"Me either, "added Tia. "There are at list fifty Guardians on site at all times. There are more than enough of us to hold the line of defense on this campus."

"But let's say that the master decided to use everything he had against us? Then what? Demons don't burn in sunlight. Neither do werewolves. We have no idea what may come and fifty Guardians with an assortment of gifts may still not be enough. She is immune to vampire bites. But what she will not be immune to yet is not a risk I am willing to take and I am sure none of you are willing to bet on it either." Eve folded her arms against her chest. Her glare, a silent dare for each one of the Guardians to challenge her on this topic, and when no one said anything, she smiled.

"Maya is not ready either," Tia grumbled, eyeing her charge with concern.

"That is because you people are afraid of what she can do," Sanaya added. "You guys brought her here with the hope that she will become an asset yet, you do not allow her to test her-"

"Her mother was a powerful Voodoo priestess Sanaya, in case you forgot. Your best friend has the ability to summon demons at will which could be-"

"To her advantage.," Eve countered. "If she can summon them, that means she has some control over them which would be helpful during a fight."

"None of this sounds like such horrible ideas," Tatsu murmured. "The most powerful gift is choice. Everyone here is capable of utilizing their God given talents to benefit the dark side. I too have questionable gifts that made my father question if he should put me out of misery." She winked at Maya before continuing. "So let us use all of our strengths for the benefit of something good instead of forcing our youth to suppress them."

Everyone began to mumble their own opinions, but it became clear that Eve's proposal made sense, Archer begrudgingly agreed to it. Sanaya still wasn't sure what all had been decided. She understood that they were going to continue her training, this time including Maya and she was almost certain that the strong Guardian potential they were talking about was King. Her stomach did backflips at the idea of his name. Tia and Lois escorted them to the gym, along with the two assassins while Eve went to retrieve the other potentials she felt would make an excellent addition to her team. Archer still had not answered her question about Halo managed to set foot on campus without torching.

Tatsu and Asim took their positions on either side of the gym, while Maya and Sanaya took a seat on the first row of the bleachers while they waited for Eve to return.

Sanaya examined her best friend closely, and for the first time since they've known each other, she noticed the confident glaze that beamed from Maya's doe like eyes. She had been recognized, and that was all she needed all along which made Sanaya smile. It was about damn Maya appreciated who and what she was. They should have done that a long time ago.

"Looks like you've got a team Naya," Maya beamed.

"It surely does and I am so glad to have my best friend forever as a part of it," Sanaya beamed back.

The two friends sat in silence, allowing their new reality to set in. *Finally,* Sanaya thought to herself. *They are going to let us actually do something.*

CHAPTER SIXTEEN

Ronan awoke in his lair, surrounded by the bodies of his victims, his body consumed with uncontrollable lust. He had not been able to make contact with is slayer in a few days, and the separation was eating away at his sanity. Smooth chocolate skin that had yet to be touched by the gentle hand of a lover; lips he desired to punish with his… in all of his 500 years of existence, no female had ever sent him into this much misery. But then again, he had never encountered a Slayer before. Her scent hadn't ripened yet, but even in its infancy, it was still enough to make him want to bury himself between her legs and never come out. She was fire…pure fire and the Guardians had her! He will level that campus to the ground if he needed to get her out. He shuddered again. Even his own palm would not ease the ache in his loins. He wondered what kind of sorcery the Guardians used to block him from her. She wasn't strong enough just yet to build a mental wall that thick to keep him out.

"It's painful isn't it?"

Ronan whipped his head around to address the intruder and when he found that it was Daemon, he materialized himself a Tom Ford business suit, and masked his victims away using illusion. He took a seat on the leather sectional, crossing his legs which did little to ease the erection that was painfully obvious.

"What are you speaking of Master?" Ronan denied coolly.

"The Slayer has gotten under your skin," Daemon cooed. "As a matter of fact, you want to fuck her so bad you can taste it. I told you to leave her be until it was time. You've been all in her head…you've tasted her fears and desires…and it doesn't help that she's a virgin that it just make the desire burn so much more doesn't it?"

When Ronan did not answer, but shuddered, Daemon chuckled.

"I don't know if I should exterminate you for disregarding my command or...if I should reward you with my assistance. That unsanctioned turned breeched their barriers, but we need to be sure that it may have something to do with the turn being unsanctioned and her Guardian traits still be recognized as a member of the Light or, that the Pope has been a very busy man in the dark realms."

Ronan tried to focus his energies on something else, like laying siege to The Academy instead of the lusty images of an underage and not fully matured Slayer but there was no use. He groaned and shamelessly moved his hand to his groin.

"You know," Daemon continued. "I honestly pity you. Really. I do. But, you foolish syncopant did you ever think about why you have not been able to commune with her even on the astral plnae?"

"Of course I have!" Ronan snapped, still stroking himself. "But, the answer eludes me."

"Perhaps because she has already found her Guardian soul mate, and his bond is blocking you."

Daemon chuckled as Ronan snarled in frustration, while at the same time copulating with the air. He shook his head as Ronan's hips thrust into the invisible lover.

"She is too young to have found such wonder," he gritted through his teeth. "Those wretched Guardians have done something to-" He shuddered as he came violently to Daemon's dismay.

"The sad part is," Daemon added. "I may not have to exterminate you myself. The Guardians will do it for me."

"I will kill each and every one of them," Ronan vowed. "She will be mine."

"Suit yourself. I have to cover my own tracks anyways and you have given me the tools to do so." Daemon turned to leave. "Do what you wish, but do not say I did not warn you."

Daemon dematerialized back to his lair Louisiana leaving the sexually frustrated and foolish vampire alone.

"She will be mine," Ronan vowed as need filled his body once again.

King had just barely gotten out of the shower when there were several loud knocks on his door. He emerged from his bathroom, a towel wrapped around his waist to answer. He was surprised to find Archer's woman, Eve and Congo standing in his doorway wearing serious expressions.

"Yeah?"

"First of all, never greet a lady with just 'yeah'," Congo said with a glare. "And second, put some clothes on. Your training begins now."

"I thought classes were cancelled," King began to protest.

"They are. But unless you prefer for another classmate to take his place by the Slayers side, then-"

King didn't let Congo finish his sentence. "I'll be dressed in five minutes."

"Make that two," Congo growled.

King closed the door and ransacked his room for a pair of jeans, Timberlands, and a loose fitting T-shirt. He emerged from his room two minutes fully dressed, and his locks hanging freely down his back. Eve took one look at him and smiled. Congo just shook his head but lead the way to the gym.

"So what's going on?" He asked Eve who walked casually by his side.

"Change. She is ready to hunt and has proven that on more than one occasion. But she cannot hunt alone. It is one of the many divine principles that surrounds the Slayer Legends and as much as all of us would love to be the ones to hunt alongside her, she needs her own team of Guardians."

"But why me? I just got here."

"I think you know why King," Eve sighed. "It has been quite obvious since you arrived that a bond has formed between the two of you. Would you rather someone else accept the job-"

"Hell no!"

"Boy, watch your language," Congo snapped without turning around.

"My bad. But no."

"Tell me young Guardian, what is it about her that draws you?" Eve kept her gaze focused ahead of them as they walked along the narrow, concrete path.

"Other than the obvious?" King began. "She's smart. Strong. She ain't like a lot of the girls from my way…She's cool, down to earth, sees what I see…she can fight…" A smile spread across his face at the image of her facing off with Halo. "Man she can fight. She isn't conceited or nothing…not out there trying to hook up with every dude that's checking for her…and she seems to be all about me."

Eve raised an eyebrow. "She seems to be about you?"

"No, she is all about me."

"Then I trust you will take your duties as her Guardian seriously," Eve stated as they arrived at the gym. She nodded to Congo who went in ahead of them. "I trust that you understand that your role as her Guardian is much more serious than the direction you two seem to be headed. She is young, 17 and will not be 18 for another few months.

Like you, she has lost a lot, and as she matures, she will lose even more. I trust that you have her best interests at heart and that you understand that you stand between the Darkness and her...and most importantly young man, I trust that because as you say, she is not like those other girls from where you are from, that you will not treat her as such."

"She's more than that," King said quietly before looking away.

"Good." Eve placed her hand on his shoulder. "You have no idea how much I needed to hear that and I believe you-until you prove me wrong. Now get in there and train. You have a lot to learn and a small window to learn it." She motioned for him to go inside before sending a silent prayer that this kid lives up to his expectations. The world needed a slayer, but as fate would have it, the slayer needed King.

∎∎

It was almost six o' clock before they were finally dismissed from training, and Sanaya could not be any more thrilled. With only four hours of sleep coupled with the grueling practices involving them fighting as a single unit, she was ready to keel over any minute. On top of all that, her heart did a million leaps in her chest the moment King walked in and smiled at her. Of course their happy reunion came to an end when Archer came and began his drills. And man were they drills...King did well holding his own when he sparred with Congo. Maya may need to go to the medical clinic to have her bruises tended to because Eve was brutal. And then there were the four other students that Eve felt would be a good fit for her team: another first year student, named Lisa; a second year student who called himself Bullet; and then there was the red haired girl named Charlie and to her dismay...Trent. Congo suggested that all of her new team members spend some time sparring with her to test her strength so that they would know and understand what kind of Guardians she would need. She tried to go easy on Maya, and her best friend held her own for a brief moment until Sanaya snapped her head back and blood lust set in; and of course Archer had to intervene. He told Maya that she is going to need tons of strength training and Pilates exercises before he felt she was strong enough to go out into the field. King managed to block a lot of her attacks, but he was no match for her speed. Trent got the snot kicked out of him. Charlie ended up unconscious. Bullet should have reconsidered a name change. And Lisa fought well...until her shoulder was dislocated. And that was just the beginning...

By the time Archer had them practicing drills where they had to work together using their abilities, things went from bad to worse. Maya's eyes started rolling to the back of her head exposing the white of her eyes and an ominous voice took over and Tatsu and Asim had to rush her to the nearby chapel to see if she needed an exorcism. Lisa-once her shoulder was popped back into place-went into a trance and Archer had to slap her a few times to get her to snap out of it. Trent proved himself valuable with his ability to mimic voices- which is a vampire trait, however, he and King kept trying to face off and Congo threatened to beat both of them unconscious if they did not pull it together. Charlie lost her opportunity to participate because she was still unconscious when it was time for the drills. And Bullet found himself tangled in his own tactical charge of energy. It was all one big catastrophe, and as Sanaya limped away with King and Eve to her room, she regretted having even approached the subject of wanting to help. She dreaded tomorrow's training.

Eve led the away, allowing them to walk side by side. King took her hand into his, and she tried not to blush.

"I missed you," He said, his voice a near whisper.

"I missed you too... you were great out there. I can tell you've had to do a lot of fighting on your own..."

"Yeah, I had to learn how to defend myself and quick," he said, his brown eyes locked onto hers. "How are you feeling? Archer and Eve kicked our asses."

Sanaya laughed. "Hell yeah they did. I knew Archer could go hard, but this time he showed no mercy."

"Is that who taught you how to fight?"

"Yup."

"You fight like a damn cage fighter shawty. Chill out on us would you?" King teased with a grin. "I thought I was in the ring with Muhammad Ali and not my girl-"

"I'm your girl?"

Her smile was so big and bright, her touch warm and inviting, King wondered how in the world did her peers not recognize her for the diamond that she is? And there was much more to her he wanted to explore; so much more that he was certain that it would take a couple of lifetimes before he managed to reach the bottom of her ocean. And she was only 17… yes he would wait for her. It was no big deal-well, it was but he could suck it up. He'd already been with a number of girls before and none of them were special. They offered and he accepted and when the time came when she decided to offer her body, her treasure as a gift to him, he would do everything in his power to honor her. So he could wait…and as a result, he may end up a better fighter.

"Yeah," He answered finally. "You are. I see that sucka Trent still trying to take you from me and that is never going to happen."

"So is this about Trent or is it-"

He silenced her question with a gentle kiss on those soft lips of hers. She gasped and silenced that too. Eve kept walking. He knew she knew but he didn't care. Whatever this was between them, he never wanted to end. She was his and always will be. At seventeen, she was old enough to choose. He could see into her mind, sense her fears, her questions…he dug a little deeper as he deepened the kiss and yes, there it was…her heart knew. She knew even when she could not articulate it she knew. He gently pulled away, blown away not only with his discovery but with the young goddess that made up Sanaya. He pulled her in close and going based on her dazed expression, he could argue that she was weak on her feet and needed the support.

"Come on you two!" He heard Eve shout from the steps of his building.

They moved as a single unit, a step up from what they were during training, moving quickly until they met Eve who stood at the top of the steps frowning.

"Listen here you two," Eve began. "Sanaya, you and I are going to have a serious heart to heart and King, I have already said my piece…" She stopped when she realized the young couple had completely tuned her out and was focused on each other's gaze, locked in a private moment.

"Oh for the love of Pete," Eve grumbled. "I will personally separate you two if-"

"Alright Eve," Sanaya muttered. "I get it."

Eve sighed and ushered both of them inside. She was kind enough to allow them a moment to say goodnight. Dinner would be served in their respective rooms to give each student time to recover from their injuries. Eve watched as King expertly kiss Sanaya once more, pulling away and taking her breath away along with it and she had to give it to the young man. He had skills. However, the last thing she needed was her Slayer distracted by the nasty little bite from the love bug. No wonder Archer wanted to kick his ass.

She watched the young couple part ways like it was the last night they would see each other and when King closed the door behind him, Eve mentally prepared herself for the conversation that was about as comfortable as a trip to the Gyno's office for a routine pelvic exam. If she didn't, then Archer would and that was the last thing either of them needed. Especially not now.

∎∎∎

Sanaya refused to think about her hour long conversation that was forced upon her by none other Eve, Tia, Lois…hell even Tatsu felt compelled to add her two cents in about sex, men, the changes taking place in her body and the dangers of her own erotic power. Things took a turn for the worse when the topic of pregnancy came about and the last thing she wanted to think about was having anyone's babies. Not now. Tia expressed that she should hold off on exploring this bond with King. She said, "Sanaya you are so young. You need to know what is out there. Never make a man your entire world." For Pete's sake she just met King! And yes, she felt things for him that went beyond a hard core crush or infatuation. There was something intimate about him being in her headspace-way more intimate than sex. Eve stressed that she needed to remain focused: King had to prove himself worthy to be her Guardian. To be her boyfriend was one thing, but to take that sacred oath to put her life above all others including himself was another. And, Eve declared that he is not just proving himself worthy to be her Guardian: he must prove himself worthy of her heart. Things really went down the crapper when they asked her about her virginity and when she admitted begrudgingly that King was the first guy she'd ever kissed, she damn near fled the room when they swooned all over the living room. Maya had just walked in when the swooning took place and she too made her cheeks burn with embarrassment.

She turned the hot water on to boiling proportions and stepped in. Her bruises had healed, but her muscles were achy and sore. Grabbing her loofa, she lathered up in the Coconut scrub before deciding to wash the sweat and grime from her wavy, shoulder length hair. Massaging the herbal Essence into her hair, she closed her eyes remembering how this brand of shampoo had been her mother's favorite. She pictured her mother, washing her hair in the kitchen sink, muscles completely relaxed as her senses indulged in the fruity scent of the popular shampoo brand. Then, she would blow dry her hair, looking every bit like Pam Grier with her fro' before she placed a hot comb to it, to straighten out the kinks and coils. It was in moments like this that she missed her mother more than anything in the world. She had no idea what happened to her aunt Francis. When her mother was killed, she was not permitted by The Vatican to come to her funeral. All contact to surviving family members came to an end and the life she once knew was over when her mother's ashes were emptied onto the hallowed ground of a local church.

Look at me mama, she thought to herself. *I am strong now. If you were alive I could protect you. I should have protected you...* One tear led to another and soon, she was standing beneath the head of the shower, Herbal Essence fused with tears rinsing down the drain. She stood underneath the flow of hot water, until her soul cried itself empty. She sniffled, rinsed her face once more and prepared to step out, when that familiar erotic presence made itself known in the dark corners of her mind. She threw up mental blocks, shielding herself but the intruder already had his foot in the door. She cut off the water, wrapped a towel around her and there she saw his image, a transparent projection of him standing in the middle of the bathroom.

"Get away from me," she growled, gripping her towel.

The vampire smiled, his green eyes lit with lust. "You are exquisite," He whispered. "Come to me! Put down your barriers slayer or-"

"Or else what?" She demanded, wishing she could put a stake in his cursed heart and be done with it.

The vampire didn't bother to respond verbally. He attacked her mind, sending her every sexual visual he owned into her mind, bringing her to her knees.

"Stop!" She groaned, fighting the urge to remove her towel and put an end to her own misery.

"Now you know what I suffer," He murmured. "But let us not suffer any longer."

Her towel came off and the entity was on top of her, struggling to break the invisible barrier that prevented him from manifesting in the flesh, when something within her snapped.

No. He would not take her against her will.

The bathroom door burst open at the same time as her eyes came a lit with bright silver and when her eyes met the master vampire's, the entity unleashed a bone chilling scream. Eve shot a series of silver tipped arrows into the hologram image only to look away in horror as he disappeared with blackened eye sockets. Sanaya remained trembling on the floor. The other Guardians rushed in, followed by Maya while Sanaya sobbed.

"He tried to…" She could not bring herself to finish the sentence as Eve wrapped her in her towel. "I don't know what happened. He was on top of me. I-"

Maya barreled into her friend's arms, sobbing with her. "He didn't take it did he?" She asked repeatedly, referring to her virginity.

"No…but I was afraid if I didn't fight harder that he would."

"Your eyes," Eve began. "You did good. Your eyes burned silver and blinded him. He's gone now…"

Tatsu in her fury flung a ginsu knife into the wall. "We couldn't get to you. He sealed you in!"

Maya and Eve helped Sanaya get dressed, while Lois called Archer, and before she tied her damp hair up, Archer, Congo Asim and a number of other male Guardians came storming in, including one everyone would least expect.

"How the fuck did that bitch get in here?" Archer shouted, pushing past his team members. "Where is he?"

"Gone. It was a projected image of himself. He was testing our barriers and he was somewhat successful," Eve explained calmly. "Her eyes burned silver and blinded him and sent him on his way."

"I'm more concerned about how he got past three Guardians and an assassin," Congo commented, studying the angry faces that glared at him.

"He had her sealed in. We couldn't get to her," Tatsu snapped. "Eve is not a full blooded vampire and even with all of our strengths, he was still too strong."

"Son of a bitch," Archer murmured.

"She is no longer safe here. The room has been compromised…"

Sanaya emerged from the bedroom, her eyes red rimmed and tear stained when she noticed the only person in the room that seemed to matter. While everyone else was talking, he approached her and took her for an embrace.

Everyone stopped talking.

"Are you alright?" King asked, wiping away residual tears that had yet to fully shed.

"Who the hell let him in here?" Archer fumed.

"He is my charge," Congo shrugged. "Where I go, he goes."

"This is not the goddamn Love Hotel!"

"Archer," Eve scolded. "Please…"

King held onto her despite Archer's threatening looks, and then once again, the voice in her head became a maddening, incessant plea to leave the campus. The voice sliced through her, prickling her skin and sending an electric current combo of pleasure fused with pain. She dropped to her knees clutching her head. King was on the ground with her, calling her. Chaos erupted around her.

"Aaaaaaaahhhhh! He's in my head!" She screamed. King pulled her into him, cradling her against his body.

"Sanaya, focus on me," King told her. "Focus on me."

Hands. Various sets of hands were on her but all she could hear was the maddening call and King's voice gaining momentum in her mind. She squeezed her eyes shut and cried out again.

"Focus on me," She heard King repeat. She felt King's presence enter her mind.

*Noooo! Get out of here! He will kill you...*she pleaded to him mentally.

Yes, tell him... the vampire taunted.

"Focus on me," King whispered to her again and this time, she saw him standing directly next to her. She reached up to touch his face and the instant his brown eyes melted into hers, everything went black...

CHAPTER SEVENTEEN

Sanaya came awake to the relaxing sounds of heavy breathing, and an even heavier arm draped across her back. She stirs, slowly becoming mentally aware that she is not alone in the room. She carefully shifts so as not to disturb whoever it was that has taken refuge in what was supposed to be her bed. She opens her eyes, and all of her senses awaken at once, alerting her to every energy signature and every scent of every individual crammed in the moderately sized bedroom that was supposed to be for her and Maya only. She gasps when she realizes that the arm once draped across her back belonged to none other than King! What was he doing in her bed? And, why would the Guardians allow it-especially Archer? She pushed a loose strand of hair from her face and studied the sleeping young, fiery man that destiny brought to her life. He slept now on his side, one arm above his head, his thick long locks blanketing his shoulders. He reminded her of a sleeping lion, nestled in the tall grass of the Serengeti. Gentle snores and deep breathes were his harmony.

She scooted over just a bit to give herself some space when she accidently bumped into a perfectly manicured foot. Maya! Her best friend was burrowed underneath a mountain of blankets, sleeping soundly. What happened? Scanning the room she noticed Congo, still strapped with a multiple Bowie knifes on his left leg holster and a Glock held firmly in his grip, while he leaned against the wall, his head nodding to the side while he dozed. Lois was sprawled out on her stomach on the floor, a stake tucked into her back. Sanaya could also sense the presence of several more Guardians nearby, and she could only imagine how many there were patrolling the halls and scaling the rooftops.

She centered her thoughts on the series of events leading up to this moment, and the last thing she remembered was the psychic attack from Ronan and then King stepping in encouraging her to focus on him. She glanced at him once more. Had he not been there, she could only imagine what would have happened. She remembered what else happened: the bathroom, Ronan on top of her...she could feel his strength, but not all of him physically. He wasn't tangible. Something blocked him from manifesting fully into corporeal form. The erotic sensations he threw off were intensely real, and she managed to get him off before...

Shaking her head, she leaned back into the cool comfort of the sheets, finding herself to be perfectly content between the two people she cared about most on the planet at this time. She could not recall everything that happened after the moment King mind locked with her, but she did know one thing: it felt great to be surrounded by people who actually had her back.

■■

King was up at first light as were the other Guardians. Sanaya, apparently was a very hard sleeper and he reasoned that it might have something to do with the changes Eve explained were taking place in her body. He kissed her gently on the top of her tussled hair, and said silent prayer of thanks that Congo allowed him to follow when she was attacked by the master vampire. The poor girl was strong, but had not reached the stage where she could mentally safeguard herself from a vampire's telepathy and was still vulnerable. Fortunately for him, he'd honed that skill years ago when he started noticing that things were changing in his old neighborhood in Atlanta. Vampires had come 'a' callin'; the youth started disappearing and violent crimes increased. He was the only kid on the block that understood what was up, and had the skills to defend himself. A female vampire rolled up on him when he was fifteen and out in the late hours hustling for some extra cash and he sensed her pull. The female was all that and then some, possessing that exotic look where identifying her race offered a challenge. He barely escaped with his life but each encounter made him stronger, and gave him the opportunity to survive both the streets and the supernatural threat that was destroying more lives than drugs and violence combined.

That was why he could get inside her mind and block the master's attempts. She needed a distraction. Besides, whenever she was around him, she became an open book. He hated leaving her, but Congo advised that his girl needed rest so that she could continue with their training. He could dig it. Besides, he needed some space to think. Plan. He needed more answers about master vampires, their abilities and what exactly she was up against. Memories of his recently abandoned life flooded his senses.

Standing on the corner of the high school he barely attended under the cover of night, he waited for the mysterious dealer to make an appearance. He already knew the deal on that fucker, and based on the number of bodies that has been disappearing since he came into town, King did not need to his heightened senses to tell him that the dealer was vampire. The plan? Exchange the package for money and be gone. The dealer's minions were vampire too, while a few of them were demons utilizing glamor to appear human. Armed with a couple of Glocks, silver chains and a couple of knives he blessed with holy water. Before his parents were murdered, they taught him and his brother well. And even though they were probably rolling around in their graves, this was survival. He still needed to eat; he had a girlfriend at home he needed to take care of; plus, he wanted to get away from the very streets he ran. A part of him wanted a better life. His girlfriend and her mother deserved a better life even though at times they could not see it for themselves. As a matter of fact, he'd asked her several times what her thoughts were on moving out of Atlanta once he saved up enough money. At the time, she tossed a thick dookie braid over her shoulder and waved her colorfully manicured hand and dismissed him as she continued reading one of her gossip magazines.

One way or another, with or without LaQuanda, he was out of Atlanta.

His crew, which consisted of three other neighborhood hustlers he grew up with waited, positioned in the shadows with guns drawn. Of course, King knew the plan was farfetched, but none of his boys believed in vampires, had never seen one and wouldn't have a clue what to do should they actually encounter a set of fangs. He could only hope that all of them would make it out of here alive, and as soon as the exchange was made, he would make himself ghost.

Shifting his weight from one foot to the other, he brushed his fingers against the Glock he held tucked in his waistband. Sweat dripped from the back of his neck down his back, courtesy of the August humidity, and his white T clung to him like second skin. His nerve endings ignited with fire as the all too familiar scent of sulfur entered his nasal passages. He spit and narrowed his gaze. A limousine pulled up, leaving it impossible for him to see beyond the tinted windows. But he didn't need to see into the tine to know what he was up against. The limo came to a stop in front of him, and he tensely waited for someone to emerge from the vehicle.

The tinted window slowly rolled down to reveal the dealer behind the deaths. His breathing slowed to deep inhales to attempt to slow down his increasing heart rate. His palms tingled with the temptation to reach for his Glock, but he kept them hanging loosely at his sides. The vampire drug lord sat relaxed against the leather interior. Don is what he called himself, but in the streets, he was known as The Black Death. Jet black hair slicked back to perfection, dark brown eyes with a hint of crimson in the center of his irises; creamy café au lait skin and dressed to the nines in a business suit. Don smiled, revealing a set of ivory fangs which led to a series of events King will never forget.

Two creatures materialized next to King, but he didn't bristled. He never moved an inch. Unfortunately, Vernon, his best friend since kindergarten shouted, "What the fuck?!" And then all hell broke loose. Cursing, King moved quickly, incapacitating one of the vampire henchmen by wrapping a silver chain around his neck, bringing the six foot entity to his knees in a screaming hiss. Gun shots rang out, and the blood curdling screams of another one of his friends was soon cut short when King heard bones snap. Several more vampires materialized from the limo, surrounding King and it was then he realized that he was going to die tonight or worse…wake up three days later feigning for blood. He would not accept the latter, so yanking out both Glocks, he went Scarface on all of them, spinning around in a circle unleashing round after round. They dematerialized and reappeared in varying spots, with the goal of forcing him to exhaust his ammo.

The package he was carrying had tumbled off into the street. Sirens were closing in and he was still in the middle of a fight for his life. He pulled the trigger as his last round of bullets finally plunged into the neck, face and chest of one of his enemies and then somehow the streetlights went out. He could hear their snarls, Don's laughter and the subtle movements of something else in the shadows before he was hit in the back of the head and collapsed onto the pavement unconscious.

He awoke to find himself handcuffed on a hospital bed and the watchful stare of Atlanta's top detective, Allen Gordon. He was facing criminal charges involving possession, conspiracy to distribute and murder. His life was about to go down the toilet in just a matter of hours when Congo, Archer and Tia walked in that day. He remembered being extremely pissed off at them for not finding him sooner and for not being there for his parents when they needed them most. As a matter of fact, he recalled being willing to face his fate with the judge instead of leaving the hospital and police custody with them. And despite his hostile protests, he went with them anyways…

And he was grateful. He found out shortly after his arrival that The Vatican had been searching for him for some time after it was discovered that his parents were murdered. Because he and his brother had no next of kin for the state to look to, they were lost in the system, which was another thing that angered him: had the courts not separated them, his brother may have lived. He would have protected him from the wrong people. He might have chosen a more positive path instead of the streets of darkness where he blossomed in his rage and anger for years. But he was here now, with a second chance to protect someone he cared about…

So, yeah he was definitely asking questions and kicking some ass during training, so the next time he found himself surrounded by a group of vamps, he would have a team with him. Sanaya would not have to fight this battle alone.

CHAPTER EIGHTEEN

"Forget everything you thought you knew," Eve began as she circled the young team of potential Guardians. "Last night, some of you witnessed a serious psychic attack conducted by a master level vampire." She listened to the surprised gasps coming from both Charlie and Lisa who were fortunate enough to not have witnessed the traumatizing event. She stopped in front of Sanaya who kept her eyes focused on the ground, muscles tenses. "It is not your fault Sanaya. We have been trying spoon feed you everything we felt you should know according to the phases typical of a Slayer. But we were wrong. You are not like the previous Slayers. We wanted to give you more time to figure out who and what you are on your own and simply guide you through the process. Again, we were wrong. There is no time." Her eyes met Archer's who stood behind the group in the gym. Eve continued to circle the teens, eyeing each one and making mental notes of their weaknesses while Archer continued the speech.

"For the last few days a master level vampire has been tracking our slayer and desperately trying to figure out a way in, and last night he was almost successful. He came in as a projected image of himself and attempted to snatch her. He banked on her being too young and not fully matured yet to activate whatever powers she has to defend herself. Slayers are not just fighters ladies and gentlemen. They are living, breathing weapons. Sanaya's scent alone is a weapon. Her blood is a weapon. She was born to hunt and kill vampires as easily as she breathes." He paused studying their faces. "And last night, she reminded the fucker just who the fuck she is."

"What did she do?" Lisa asked glancing at Sanaya.

"We are not sure how she did it, but Eve says her eyes burned bright silver and burned the bastard's retinas out. He fled before she could finish him off."

A sense of awe blanketed the room and now all eyes were on Sanaya.

"But that's not everything," Archer continued. "Sanaya was able to get him off of her, but that did nothing but piss him off even more. He attacked her again mentally, which all vampires are capable of doing. He forced himself into her mind with the goal of driving her out of the safety of the group with his call. Had it not been for King, it would have been one hell of a night for the Slayer."

Now all eyes were on King, with Maya offering a knowing smirk. He shot a glance to Eve who simply smiled at him which made him stand a little taller.

"I am telling you this because even though all of you are highly gifted, you still need each other's backs. It is important for you to be aware of one another's strengths and weaknesses but one of you might be person who either saves your teammate's life or be the cost of it. For instance, we all know Maya can summon demons at will and has proven to be a strong Clairvoyant. Summoning demons is a bit of a struggle for Guardians to accept, but think of the possibility. Imagine all of you trapped in a known hell cavern surrounded by legions of demons. Eight against thousand, you figure out the odds. With her ability to summon, she can also control them which may give you enough time in your fight to get the hell out of dodge." Archer shrugged. "Just sayin…"

"And Charlie is no slouch either," Eve added. "Telekinesis is her talent. She can manipulate all forms of matter with her mind. So if the day comes when it is raining bullets, she can project a force field around you. Just like with all of your gifts, the possibilities are endless."

"Lisa is our other fighting machine," Archer stated planting a firm palm on her shoulder. Lisa's slanted eyes surveyed the group around her nervously. "Don't be shy about your gifts Lisa. You are the group's Seer. You can look into past and present events and paired with Sanaya the both of you can warn the group of pending doom or look to the past for answers to present questions. Plus, the girl has moves like Jet Li in action."

Lisa's grin widened when Archer moved next to King who eyed him suspiciously. "And this is our diamond in the rough," He added evenly. "This guy came onto campus already equipped with experience from fighting vamps and demons. Not only can he sense them like our Slayer, but he can smell them-which I may add, sucks. This guy is a strong Clairvoyant which is how I suspect he managed to back that master off of Sanaya. Plus, he has some tactical energy in palms he can manipulate. If any of you want someone to have your back other than Sanaya, this would be your guy."

"And let's not forget about Trent," Eve said approaching the young man with a grin. "He is our audio who can hear a pin drop a mile away. Not only that, he operates like a reverse audio which you all witnessed him do when he threw his voice across the gym which confused all of you. In a fight that can come in handy when you are targeting a vampire or a werewolf."

"Last but not least," Archer said as he approached the kid everyone called Bullet. The twitchy kid bounced from foot to foot, his blue eyes lit with anticipation as the group faced him. "This is our superhero. He may be faster than Sanaya, but that won't be determined until I clock them. Last time I checked, Bullet can reach speeds of one hundred miles per hour. He can outrun the fastest land mammal on the planet with ease. Honestly, we have never seen anything or anyone like him but the problem is, he can only maintain that speed for a short period of time before his body threatens to overheat...Sanaya requires some time to build her speed and she does not utilize it as often as she should. Bullet, on the other hand is twitchy as hell. It's almost as if he is required to move at that speed constantly just to keep his organs functioning properly." Archer offered the lanky boy a grin along with a power bar which he greedily accepted. "Now that you all know who and what each other can offer to the team, start acting like a team. Bullet could be useful in a rescue mission when seconds count. Help each other to grow and expand your gifts. This is the first time a Guardian team has been assembled before the Slayer decides who she wants on her team. Prove us right that you deserve your position because we have a hundred other students to choose from. Understand?"

When the group mumbled in agreement, Eve, Tia, Archer, Congo, Tatsu and Asim lined up in front of them wearing serious expressions.

"Now let us begin," Eve growled as her fangs lengthened.

■■

Petronius smiled as he watched from his HD 60" flat screen the master vampire known as Ronan moan in pain as he fed from another victim hoping to repair his eyes. The damage was done. Silver burned his eye sockets to mush and it would not matter how much he fed, his eyes could never be repaired. The poor bastard might as well step out into the sun and allow daylight to finish him off. Taking a seat on his leather office chair, he reclined to face the moonless night sky view from the twenty fifth floor vantage point, remembering the days of old when vampires were worshipped like gods and could roam the infant cities and streets freely until the day the very first Slayer stepped onto the scene. Since then, vampires and all supernatural entities alike had to retreat to the shadows where they have operated ever since, and it will not be until a day walker is born that the offense of the sun may be remedied.

Alex was supposed to be here for their meeting. Daemon had not been invited as it were discovered that his dear and ambitious brother had other plans of his own. The Beast had called a meeting to discuss the future of the vampire race and what their plans were to deal with the new Slayer. Smoothing out the lapels of his blood red suit jacket, he misted into the atmosphere to the second tenth floor where the board room was located to find The Beast, disguised as a human from European descent, dressed in a black Tom Ford exclusive suit, with his chestnut brown hair slicked back exposing his handsome features seated at the head of the table. Alex materialized soon after opting for the tuxedo and bow tie look, as if he were on his way to a ball. The

Beast scowled as soon as the vampire took a seat across from Petronius.

"Did you be sure to drop the princess off at midnight?" The Beast murmured with narrowed eyes.

"Actually, there is a blood bath ball over in New Orleans tonight," Alex chirped. "Humans have organized the event with the hope that immortality would be offered as a gift from members of our kind. I thought I might attend."

"Humans should not be aware that we even exist unless they happen to fall victim to one of our encounters," Petronius snapped.

"Ah, but these are no ordinary humans-witches, I might add." Alex began to cough and sputter up blood which he hacked on the floor to The Beast's dismay.

"I could have healed you," said The Beast. "It would have cost you several hard bargains and half of your life, but I would have healed you none the less. However, any vampire that is foolish enough to find himself stabbed by a blessed blade by a Guardian nonetheless deserves his fate. You are proof that I made a serious error in selecting the vampire race as my true heirs."

"Which is why we are here to discuss our plans to rebuild the race, Your Majesty," Petronius added quickly.

The Beast relaxed against the office chair, and offered Petronius a sly grin exposing several rows of sharp pointed teeth. "Enlighten me."

"We have located the Slayer. She is approximately four years away from maturity and we have already implemented a strategy to weaken her resolve in preparation for phase two of our plan-"

"Let me guess," The Beast leaned forward, creating a tent with his hands. "You want to attempt to make another day walker. That is your plan to rebuild the vampire nations and to give me reason to sanction turn bites. Am I correct or am I so far off the field I need an escort to find my way back?"

When neither vampire spoke, The Beast laughed. "As old as you are Petronius, you still have dreams of building a day walker empire. Well, I hate to break it to you my son, but I have the power to turn both of you into day walkers. You don't need to sire with a whore of Light to do so. But you two idiots have done little to strengthen my cause. Sure I'd love to see her broken and every Guardian around the world either dead or on their knees begging me for life, but I have much bigger fish to fry. This is a new millennium gentlemen. I will sanction the turn bites because I need an army. Hell, I give you full permission to target every Guardian detected until there are none left. Turn them into the very thing in which they hunt. I will align you with the werewolf clans to strengthen your numbers until we have enough vampires to turn nighttime hours into a field of nightmares. But I want you to do something for me..."

Petronius swallowed thickly because when The Beast made a request one delivered...or suffered the extremely painful consequences.

"There is an entity that has been around for almost as long as I and when I say he is long lived and hard to kill, believe it. He wears a mark that offers a ward of protection from his enemies. He is on the path seeking redemption, and after the shit he's done well, I seriously doubt the Light will even consider giving him a second chance, and I am not even talking about that little incident when he killed his brother. Find him. I need him our side. His blood is valuable as his allegiance."

"Who is it?" Alex whispered.

The Beast stood up, straightened his tie and smiled coolly. "Cain."

"But-"

The Beast disappeared before Petronius could finish his sentence.

Petronius and Alex shared an uneasy glance.

"The Beast wants us to locate the father of all vampires?" Alex wheezed in horror.

"It appears that he does," Petronius added grimly.

"What have we done dear brother?" Alex buried his face in his hands. "What have we done?"

CHAPTER NINETEEN

Sanaya collapsed in the middle of the gym floor bloodied and bruised like the rest of her teammates. The Guardians once again proved to be extremely formidable and she mentally kicked herself for ever doubting them. But her team proved to have some potential. Lisa kicked serious ass today when she went against Tatsu. It was like watching lightening in motion. The Japanese student showed little fear and when Eve slammed her into the gym floor, creating a small splinter, Lisa flipped off her back and went after her again. When she was too busy blocking punches from both Archer and Congo, King had her back when Asim moved on her with feline agility and hit him with the tactical energy supercharged by Bullet and knocked him out of the way. Charlie and Maya fought well together against Eve, when she turned her attentions against them. The two moved as a unit as they tag teamed Eve with kicks and punches and when Charlie lifted Maya for a spin, Sanaya watched with amazement as her best friend landed multiple kicks to Eve's face, neck and abdomen before Charlie finished her off with an uppercut. It was gloriously brutal. Eve stumbled back before she collapsed, but when she sat up, she gave the girls two thumbs up.

Everyone fell silent when Sanaya faced off with Tatsu after Lisa had taken a hit which left dazed on the floor. The assassin's name alone meant "dragon" and the fierce fighter demonstrated how dragon like she could be. She used a series of telepathic hits that sent Sanaya flying into the brick plastered wall of the gym. Slightly dazed and disoriented, Sanaya was on her feet before she could blink, eyes burning silver and enveloped in complete and total fury. She snatched a long blade from the table near the bleachers and Tatsu matched her with a sword in each hand, illustrating her dexterity. Sanaya could dig it. She would learn how to use both hands in a fight soon enough. Tatsu was not nearly as fast as Sanaya but she was much more agile and managed to dodge a number of her swings, until Sanaya sliced Tatsu's swords in half like butter. In the far corner of her mind, Sanaya could sense the need for blood spill over into her psyche and that is when she knew

Tatsu was in trouble. Unfortunately, there was not a thing she could do to turn it off. She could hear Archer and Eve screaming her name. And then someone else stepped in. Eve. And she fought them too. It wasn't until Archer hit her with a blow from behind, right in the center of her spine that she collapsed onto the floor, exhausted.

Thankfully, Tatsu had just been knocked unconscious, suffering only a few bone fractures. Breathing hard, bloody and aching in various parts of her body, Sanaya shook off what was left of blood lust before attempting to stand. Today was brutal. King and Bullet offered their hands to help her onto her feet.

"You all did very well today," Archer said breathing heavily. "Sanaya, we still need to work on guarding your mind and exercising control of the bloodlust. But, I'm proud of you Slayer. I'm proud of all of you. Let's head on over to the dining hall so we can grub."

Everyone mumbled in agreement and while Archer led the way with Congo and Eve trailing behind, Sanaya walked arm in arm with King. Maya, naturally found her way to her best friend's side, as did Charlie, Lisa and Bullet.

"It is a pleasure to fight with you," Lisa said softly to Sanaya. "You have no idea how much of an honor it is to me and my family."

"Aww thanks Lisa," Sanaya chirped. "Same here. It feels good to…have a team."

"We bled together so that makes us fam now," Maya added swinging her arm around Charlie.

King gently kissed Sanaya on top of her head. "Damn shawty, remind me to never piss you off."

"You don't have to worry about that King," Sanaya whispered. "Please don't. None of you don't have to worry-"

"We know," Charlie added offering Sanaya a smile. "We've heard about you. It was awesome seeing you in action."

"Well, where was all the love before?" King demanded. Sanaya sent a silent thank you to him for asking the one thing she's thought since Eve placed all of them together.

"We never got to see for ourselves how awesome you are," Bullet shrugged. "Elizabeth told everyone that you were a psychopath who could barely control her powers and that incident with Ryder didn't help."

"Well that was stupid as hell to judge someone without getting to know them," King mumbled.

"We are sorry for judging you," Charlie replied solemnly. "I should have come to sit with you and see for myself instead of believing a girl who uses bullying to get her way."

"Same here Sanaya," Bullet added, offering his hand. "We are a team now, so we stick together."

Maya and Charlie gave each other a pound, while the rest of the group huddled together, with the exception of Trent who remained a few paces behind and quietly withdrawn into his thoughts.

When the group made it to the dining hall, Bullet took it upon himself to snag two tables and push them together, while everyone grabbed their trays. All eyes were on them as they chattered away like old friends. Even Elizabeth's table watched them curiously. Sanaya took a seat with King to her left and Maya seated to her right next to Charlie, and Lisa and Bullet facing them. Their jovial spirit diminished the moment, King noticed Trent taking a seat with Elizabeth and her harem.

"Wow," King said still glaring in his direction. "I guess ol' boy made his choice."

"I guess so," Sanaya agreed.

"Remind me not to have his back," Bullet mumbled.

"Maybe Elizabeth put a spell on him," Lisa added.

"Elizabeth has no skills whatsoever in anybody's magical arts," Maya replied sharply. "She is about as useful as a regular Joe. The only thing she has to offer is money."

"Well maybe that is what he is after," Charlie mumbled.

"Let's not worry about him guys," Sanaya said finally after taking a bite of her chicken Alfredo. "Like King said, he's made his choice. He is still a member of our team and he will eventually find out what kind of person Elizabeth is."

The group ate in silence, with King and Sanaya exchanging a few mental caresses here and there, and when it was time to leave Sanaya felt Elizabeth's hateful sneer at her back. She turned around and smiled out of spite before tossing her tray on the cart. Nothing was going to spoil this day. Nothing.

■■■

Something was wrong. Sanaya could not place her finger on it, but she knew it in her bones that something wasn't right either. The Guardians had placed a barrier around her room so that if the master found a way to recover he would not be capable of successfully completing another attack. Stepping out of the shower, she listened to Charlie giggle with Maya about a time she tripped Elizabeth with her own shoe laces. King was in his own unit with Bullet. He'd sent her a text message earlier making sure she was ok and promising to convince Congo to allow him time to see her. She smiled at the thought.

She spent the next hour straightening her hair with an electric hot comb and fat iron until it left a silky, dark path down her shoulders. As soon as her monthly stipend came in, she was ordering some hair so she could maintain the braids she desperately needed. Emerging from the bathroom freshly showered and hair manageable, she still struggled to shake the nagging feeling that something was amiss. Lois and Myra had switched shifts with Eve after Archer had given the OK for Charlie and Lisa to spend the night with them. Lisa had yet to be escorted by one of the other Guardians. She tightened the draw string on her pink pajama bottoms and wrapped a silk scarf around her head and took a seat on the edge of the bed closest to the window. Her skin prickled.

"Are you alright Sanaya?" Charlie asked, tying her thick mane of red hair into a ponytail. "You look...stressed."

"I don't know. Something isn't right," Sanaya murmured glancing at the window. "Maybe I'm being paranoid."

"Well the Guardians took extra measures to barricade the room against the vampire now that they have a name," Maya added gently.

"I know. It's just-"

A hard blast shook the building, knocking Sanaya off the bed and onto the floor. Lois and Myra burst into the room, guns drawn.

"Stay here," Lois commanded. "The campus is under attack!"

Sanaya could hear the mental SOS Archer sent out to every available Guardian, requesting that they abandon their posts and man positions around the cardinal points of the school. They were indeed under attack. Sanaya was on her feet instantly, expanding her mental awareness to what was taking place just outside the Vatican. Dark clouds blanketed the sky and streak after streak of black lightening flashed as the howls of werewolves echoed in the atmosphere. Hell caverns splintered the ground and opened, allowing legions of dark forces the luxury of escape. Sanaya took one look at her two friends, before running past them to switch her pink pajama bottoms into a pair of denim jeans and Timberland boots.

"The Guardians said for us to stay here," Charlie pleaded, looking at Sanaya as if she lost her mind.

"And do what?" Sanaya snapped as she laced up her boot "Wait for us to die? This is what we are being trained for-" Suddenly she was hit with the familiar call from none other than Ronan. She collapsed on her knees and covered her ears to blot out the high frequency of the call. Her body shivered from the erotic pull but she fought against it, focusing on King.

You will pay for what you've done to me. I will kill every single one of your peers as you writhe on the ground begging for my pleasure, Ronan threatened.

"Sanaya!" Maya cried as she dropped on the ground to help her friend.

Sanaya heard her, but now Ronan was showing her images of The Guardians on the front lines fighting. He sent a small army of freshly turned vampires who slaughtered their way through the Vatican, leaving blood and carnage behind them. The Church's assassins were fighting with everything they had with every ability and skill at their disposal.

"He wants a fight," Sanaya gritted through her teeth. "You guys are now a part of the most elite fighting team in the world," she challenged. "Fight with me, or get out of my way."

Maya was up on her feet donning a similar outfit as Sanaya: jeans and Timberlands. Sanaya reached for her buzzing cell and answered quickly. "Yeah?"

"'Naya'," came King's voice. "What's up? We riding with you or what? You see that shit outside? Congo was like 'stay inside' and I'm like hell no."

"I'm already dressed. Meet us in the courtyard. Turn anything and everything into a weapon. And last but not least," she lowered her voice. "Be careful."

"I will baby. You too." She disconnected the call to find Charlie and Maya waiting for her.

"Underneath the floorboards in the kitchen are weapons. There is a safe behind the painting, and I am counting on you, Charlie, as a Seer to crack the code. I think there may be weapons in there too. Break off the legs of the dining room chairs to make stakes. Everything is a weapon."

Sanaya rushed to the floorboards while Charlie worked on the safe.

"There are demons," Maya said flatly standing behind her.

Sanaya quit working for a second to face her friend. "I know. But that is what we have you for."

"I don't know if I can control them Naya. And what if that turns me evil?"

Sanaya stood from her low crouch and hugged her friend. "You are my best friend Maya. Nothing can make you evil. You can do this."

"But what if I can't?" Maya sniffled, burying her face into Sanaya's shoulder.

"You can because you can and I believe in you. I need you to believe that, ok?"

Maya slowly pulled away and wiped her eyes. "I can do this."

Sanaya smiled. "Yes you can."

They returned to the task of collecting weaponry which included: several light grenades, a crossbow which Sanaya handed to Charlie along with the silver tipped arrows; several bowie knives and a couple of 9 mm; a mini Uzi; and all Charlie found from the safe were small bottles of what Sanaya assessed to be Holy Water.

It was absolute chaos once they stepped outside. Students were fleeing in every direction while others tried to take a stand. Some of the older students fought back to back with a couple of Guardians but the campus had been completely overrun. The three girls found King and Bullet working in tandem against a werewolf that decided he wanted to come out and play. Sanaya flung a silver tipped knife into its back and watched the creature howl in pain before disintegrating into ash. The five friends took formation as Sanaya handed King and Bullet an Uzi, a hand held, and some bottles of holy water. With Sanaya positioned in front of them she led them through the darkness as they took down vampire after wolf followed by demon upon demon.

"There are too many of them Sanaya!" Maya called out as she dropped to the ground and tripped the wolf that lunged at Charlie, who then spun around and connected her foot to its jaw.

"Maya! You know what you can do! We can take care of the vampires and the wolves but the demons are endless!" Sanaya called out to her with eyes burning silver. "Tap into that part of you that calls them!" Sanaya's head snapped back and she unleashed a battle cry as bloodlust took over. From the corner of her mind's eye she saw what a true demon summoner looked like. Maya's eyes took on a white glow, as her long braid levitated from her shoulder. Lightening crackled above her forcing King, Bullet and Charlie to step back.

Sanaya unloaded several silver rounds into another wolf, as Maya began to chant in an ancient language that probably had yet to be discovered by today's archaeologists. The already blackened sky seemed to grow darker, and the only one capable of seeing through it was Sanaya. She kicked, shot and blasted her way back to her team to protect them from the temporary vulnerability as legions of grotesquely formed entities surrounded Maya awaiting her command.

"Send them back!" Sanaya shouted as she grabbed King, who held onto Charlie whose hand latched onto Bullet's as they ran for cover. Sanaya could still hear Maya's chant that was followed by a sonic blast that sent the screaming, resentful demons back into the Hell caverns from which they came. Guardians, students and vampires alike stopped fighting to witness the event in shock. The demonic screams shattered glass windows, and for those with sensitive hearing, they collapsed on the ground with bleeding ears. When it was done, Maya fainted and Bullet rushed to her side before her head hit the ground.

"Take her to the church!" Sanaya yelled as more fighting began. Bullet nodded and whizzed off.

"What are you-" Archer demanded as he approached carrying a bloodied ax before he was hit with a black charge in the center of his chest, knocking him unconscious.

"Archer!" Sanaya shouted as she dashed to his aid. She reached his unconscious body before Tia and Myra did, and checked his pulse. He was still alive, but barely.

"Slayer!" A thunderous roar rocked the entire campus, sending the remaining vampires running.

"Sanaya, we've got to take you to safety," Lois declared, taking hold of her arm. Sanaya pulled away.

"No. No more running. He is weak. I can sense his energy dipping. Plus, he is blind. His eyes never recovered...I can take him," Sanaya said spinning around and running at full speed towards the vampire.

She could hear Guardians and her teammates alike begging her to come back. But she would not be deterred. This was her fight. No one was going to get in her way.

She found the entity standing just beyond the fountains in front of the school. She was right. His eye sockets never healed. Instead of the perfect blue eyes that once blazed with lust, were dark puddles of oozing black blood. Ronan faced off with her and smiled. Six inch fangs greeted her, along with a massively built body. Cracking his knuckles, he circled her. She kept her eyes on him, never once giving him her back.

"We could end this if you leave with me, Slayer," He murmured. "Do not allow my blindness to dissuade you although you will pay extensively for what was done to me."

"Never. Going. To. Happen," she growled, palming the butt of the hand held that she tucked in her waistband.

"Foolish girl. Guns don't scare me," He taunted.

"I don't expect them to," She challenged, still watching him.

"I am so going to enjoy fucking you, right after I rip out the throat of the Guardians that have evidently done a piss poor job of protecting you."

"Not on your life," She growled as she flung a bowie knife into the center of his chest, which he caught with both hands.

"Nice try," He chuckled before dematerializing into mist and appearing behind her with his arm wrapped around her neck.

Instead of resisting him, she went perfectly still, giving him the false sense of having the upper hand. But when his hot tongue ran a trail down her neck, her eyes burned pure silver and she flipped him onto his back with little effort. Dazed, but not totally defeated, the vampire was on his feet. She could hear gun fire, and even saw a few bullets whiz pass her face and into the entities chest. They weren't silver, so all they would do is hold him off for a few seconds. Good. The Guardians had her back. She double backed and used the fence as leverage for her to flip and land a couple of kicks to his face. He stumbled and at the same time made a grab for her, which he missed. Focusing on her rage, her eyes sent a laser of silver in his direction and she blasted him in the center of his chest. The stench of sulfur and blood filled her nostrils and his mournful screams echoed throughout the campus. She heard someone call her name. It was Tatsu and she tossed Sanaya her long blade which fell effortlessly into her grip.

"Do you know why I was able to breach the safety of your walls?" Ronan wheezed.

Sanaya slowly approached him, gripping the long blade tightly.

"More are coming," He threatened. "They seek you with the same desperation that I have sought you"

"Shut up," Sanaya finally said as she raised the blade high above her head.

"Your Guardians are not who you think they are. Neither is your Pope-"

His head rolled onto the grass as the rest of his body combusted into flames. She watched with disgust as his head followed suit before dropping to her knees. Guardians and her teammates surrounded her. Eve placed a gentle hand on her shoulder.

"You did very well Slayer. It is done. Let's finish kicking vampire and werewolf ass and take back our campus."

The battered and beaten group all cheered as Sanaya rose to her feet with the long blade in hand.

"Let's do this."

■■

CHAPTER TWENTY

By dawn the campus was demon, werewolf and vampire free, but Sanaya knew that the battle that they fought was far from over. This was only the beginning. Several students had to be put down after sustaining vampire bites and too far into the transition to risk attempting to save. Multiple Guardians were seriously injured and had to be rushed off to the Vatican Hospital for treatment, and those that remained assisted with the cleanup and figuring out what needed to be repaired along with the funeral details for those awaiting angelic transport into the Light. Archer eventually gained consciousness but would require a lengthy stay in the hospital before the doctors would permit him back on patrol. Eve and Congo would be in charge for the time being. And as for the missing students, a memorial was scheduled to be held in a few days, their bodies having been spotted among the masses of vampires and werewolves.

The school would be closed for an indeterminate amount of time, until things could be sorted out as to who was responsible for weakening prayer lines and the hallowed grounds to permit the worse attack in The Academy's history on campus grounds. Students with living family were sent home, while those with nowhere else to go were permitted to either stay or be transported to foster Guardian homes temporarily. Sanaya decided to stay as did the rest of her team. She was able to sigh with relief when she found out Lisa was ok. She'd been trapped on the first floor of her building during the invasion and could not find her way out. Guardians had to dig her out, and thankfully minus a few scrapes and bruises, she was fine.

Maya recovered, eventually awaking to receive a round of applause by the Guardians, Sanaya and their new friends. The doctors said she may suffer from severe migraines for a while, but that was better than not having her best friend back. Maya proved she can control her power. Life was good, for now, and Sanaya would not have it any other way. Before leaving her friend in the hospital room to finish recovering,

Sanaya hugged her with everything she had, and made a silent vow to herself to keep that burning flame of hope alive and well among her friends because that was what they needed to get through the darkest of nights.

As for Trent, during the battle, he and Elizabeth found themselves cornered by several vampires and barely escaped with their lives. Had it not been for his ability to throw his voice, and a nearby Guardian that tossed a light grenade in their direction, giving them ample time to escape. Afterwards, Elizabeth attempted to lie about who scored the victory and saved the day, which forced Trent to rethink his alliance with the petty blonde.

Sanaya, King, Charlie, and Bullet were seated in the semi empty dining hall when Trent approached them with his tray. All four turned to face him curiously.

"Ay, may I sit here?"

"No traitors allowed at this table," King growled. "Loyal members only."

"He is still a member of our team," Charlie added with a shrug. "And we still have to treat him like so."

No one bothered to respond as Trent took a seat next to Bullet, who refused to acknowledge his presence. The group just continued to eat in silence, until Charlie and Bullet retreated to their rooms and Trent excused himself to speak with one of the Guardians, leaving King alone with Sanaya.

"We are finally alone boo," King said with a smile.

"I know. We better treasure this moment while we can," Sanaya added with a smirk.

"Come here," King said turning around to face her.

Sanaya leaned forward thinking he was going to kiss her and when he didn't she sat back, feeling confused.

"I wanted to ask you something," He said looking every bit of anxious as he sounded.

"Go ahead."

"Sanaya, I never met a girl like you…for real for real you are everything I never thought I would have. I didn't ask you properly and I know you was cool with it but I just wanted-"

"Yes King?"

"-to know if you would officially be my girl?"

Sanaya's eyes met his and she loved the way she lost herself in the deep pools of chocolate brown that stared back at her and through her. Everything she experienced while at The Academy was new, and this journey with King would be no different. No guy had ever made her feel the way that King did and she doubted that any guy ever would.

"Yes King. I would love to officially be your girl."

King leaned in and sealed the deal with a kiss to blow her mind, but she ended up blowing his. Her soft and full lips and her gentle caress as she wrapped her arms around his neck reminded him that despite her ferocious warrior abilities, she was still a young woman who needed to be handled with care. The two pulled away when they sensed the presence of Guardians approaching, but they held on to each other as they knew they always would.

"Alright love birds," Congo shouted with a wink. "Back to the dorms. Training is still taking place tomorrow. One monkey don't stop no show."

As King took his tray and hers too, for the first time ever in Sanaya's life she knew that whatever battles she fought, regardless of how many, and throughout whatever circumstances she went through, he would always have her back.

If you are looking down from On High mom, she thought to herself as she took King's hand while Congo escorted them back to their rooms, *Just know that I love you and will always love you.*

Stepping outside into the late evening breeze a blue butterfly flitted past Sanaya and she could have sworn she heard the pretty insect say, "*I love you too baby…Mama is watching out for you.*"

Stay tuned for the next book in The Vampire Hunters Academy…The Shadows…

Made in the USA
San Bernardino, CA
21 December 2016